ONLY THE DEAD

WARREN WHITMIRE

PROLOGUE

Fayetteville, North Carolina
September 9, 2008

Detective Derek Ballinger rested his right hand on his Glock as the sound of footsteps grew nearer. He hitched up his baggy sweatpants and peered into the shadows of the hot Carolina night. A mosquito buzzed toward him, and Ballinger shooed it away with his left hand. When a teenaged boy in an oversized football jersey emerged from the shadows, Ballinger sighed and let his arms fall to his sides. The boy bopped toward Ballinger, advancing between rows of moldering clapboard houses that faced each other like ranks of soldiers braced for battle.

"Here comes the Candyman," Ballinger said, brandishing a toothy grin.

"I told you I had this, DB," the boy said, smiling back.

"Yeah, you did. I hope you did some good work tonight."

They looked up as a dark blue Ford Crown Victoria crawled to a stop beside them, its headlights turned off. Candyman's eyes were glued to the car while Ballinger checked his watch. The car door opened, but the dome light did not come on. A lean, muscular man stepped out, left the engine running, and walked toward Ballinger and Candyman.

"Hey, Detective Agosto," Candyman said. "I told y'all I got this. Ain't that what I said?"

"That's what you said, all right," the man replied. "And what did *I* say? I said, 'don't call me Detective Agosto in public. Call me Gus.'"

Candyman laughed.

"You know what comes next," Ballinger said. "Let's make it quick."

Candyman raised his arms while Ballinger and Agosto searched him. Agosto removed a small plastic bag from Candyman's pants pocket.

"Approximately two grams of what appears to be methamphetamine," Agosto said. He took the bag to the back of the Crown Vic, opened the trunk, and dropped it into a sandwich-sized plastic evidence bag. While Agosto labeled the bag with a marker, Ballinger unspooled a length of wire from Candyman, who held his shirt up and turned a slow circle.

"Dealer's a tall skinny white dude," Candyman said. "Blue jeans, cowboy shirt, just hanging around under the streetlight." After turning a full circle, Candyman reached into his jeans and pulled out a box the size of a key fob. Agosto took the box and the length of wire, put them into a separate bag and eased the trunk shut.

"But there's something off with this guy," Candyman said.

"Something's off, huh?" Ballinger asked. "He acting crazy?"

"No."

"Twitchy?"

"Naw, more like ... like he's too healthy to be a doper, and he's not one of the Gs from McFadden Street. Kinda scary the way he looks at you."

"Yeah, whatever," Ballinger said. He smiled and patted Candyman on the shoulder. "Good work, young man."

"So, we're even now?" Candyman asked.

Ballinger shrugged. "Depends on who this guy is. If he's a big enough fish, our relationship ends here." Then he gave Candyman a stern, fatherly look. "Whatever happens, you need to straighten up and fly right. Mess up one more time and you're gonna be in too deep for me to help you. Understand?"

"Oh yeah," Candyman said, still grinning. "Straight A's in school and front pew in church with my grandma every Sunday. I got this."

"I sure hope so," Ballinger said.

"Later, Detective Agosto," Candyman said before slipping back into the night.

Agosto shot the young man an irritated glance but said nothing.

As soon as Candyman had rounded the corner, Ballinger glanced at his watch again and then checked the position of his shoulder holster.

"Something wrong, boss?" Agosto asked. "You're acting nervous."

"I don't know, Gus," Ballinger said, looking around. "Candyman don't spook easy, but he said our man is scary. Could mean nothing, could be bad news. You be careful."

"You got it, boss," Agosto said. He hitched up his gun belt, climbed back into the Crown Vic, and pulled onto the road, his headlights still off. As it pulled away, Ballinger patted the car's rear quarter panel and let his hand linger for a second. His eyes stayed locked onto the car as it slipped into the darkness. He hitched up his sweatpants again and trotted down the sidewalk with an occasional glance around him.

Two blocks down, Ballinger watched as the Crown Vic slid into the greenish, lunar glow of the streetlight. A figure stood in the cone of light, looking almost like an actor on stage – tall, lean, and alert.

"Don't run," Ballinger whispered, "and don't draw down on us. Go easy."

Just then, Agosto flipped on the headlights, causing the man to shield his eyes. Agosto pulled to the curb and sprang out, his left hand on his belt, beside his badge, and his right suspended just over the grip of the Glock 17 in his hip holster.

Ballinger sped up.

"Evening," Agosto said.

"Evening, officer," the man replied, his tone cool and his body language neutral.

Agosto paused and cleared his throat. "Live around here?"

"Yeah."

"Where?"

"Nearby."

"Um hmm," Agosto said, nodding. His right hand trembled and rested on the Glock.

The man stood completely still, but his eyes followed Agosto's hand. "Is there a problem, officer?"

Agosto ignored the question. "What you selling?"

"I don't have to answer that."

Ballinger entered the streetlight's cone. "No, but you might as well," Ballinger said. The man turned toward Ballinger, who stepped into the light, his left hand cupping his badge and his right hand beside his pistol. "We're gonna find out when we search you."

"On the ground. Lay down slowly," Agosto said. "Keep your hands where I can see them."

The man raised his hands, knelt, and then lay in a prone position.

"You got any weapons on you or anything else you want to tell me about?" Agosto asked.

"Negative," the man responded. "Don't need them right now. Am I under arrest?"

"Depends on what I find when I search you."

The man offered no resistance as Agosto cuffed and searched him. Agosto smiled as he pulled a woman's makeup kit out of the man's hip pocket.

"I'm guessing there ain't no lipstick in that," Ballinger chuckled.

Agosto opened the makeup case, pushed aside a wad of cash, and extracted a plastic sandwich bag. He held it up in the beam of the Crown Vic's headlights.

"Look at this, boss!"

"Now, where would a nice young man like you get a half ounce bag of meth?" Ballinger asked.

"Boss, that's nearly an ounce or I'll buy you a beer."

"Where'd you get this?" Ballinger asked again.

"Every product originates with a producer," the man said, as if explaining an obvious truth to a child. "Then it moves through a distribution network."

Agosto looked quizzically at Ballinger.

"This ain't your turf, son," Ballinger said with a laugh. "Lucky we found you before the McFadden Street Gs came along." He looked at Agosto and nodded.

"Yeah. Why on earth are you dealing out here?" Agosto asked.

"I'll tell you if—"

"Hold on, cowboy," Ballinger interjected. "Save your bargaining for when we take you to the station and read you your Miranda rights."

Two minutes later, Agosto shoved the blue-eyed man into the back seat of the Crown Vic as Ballinger settled into the front passenger seat. Ballinger smirked at the man in the rear-view mirror. "You got no ID on you. What's your name?"

"Does it matter?" the man said. "Besides, you're not really looking for drugs, are you? You're looking for a man."

"Exactly," Agosto said with a glance at the rear-view mirror. "And when I see you back there wearing matching bracelets, I'd say we got one." He and Ballinger laughed.

"I'm not the man you're looking for, and we all know it," the man said.

Ballinger stopped laughing. "What do you know about the man we're looking for?"

"His house, his habits, his friends. How he's kept one step ahead of you for so long."

Ballinger shivered despite the heat. "Tell us about it at the station."

"You take me to the station and Mirandize me, and I won't tell you anything. On the other hand, you work with me, and I'll tell you everything you need to know to take down Voodoo."

"Voodoo?" Agosto asked. "Did somebody tell you that's who we're gunning for?"

"Doesn't matter how I know. I just know. You want to take down Voodoo."

Ballinger turned and studied the man in silence. The Crown Vic glided past a stretch of overgrown lots punctuated by rusty "for sale" signs and rotting mobile homes.

"What's your game, son?" Ballinger asked. "Besides keeping yourself out of prison, why would you want to help us take down Voodoo?"

The blue-eyed man studied Detective Ballinger for a long moment, his face blank and his shoulders relaxed even though his hands were cuffed.

"Does it matter?"

1

Major Hank McCaskill smiled as he stepped off the UH-60 helicopter and onto the searing concrete of the airstrip. *I'm almost done with this heat.* He gripped his M-4 carbine with his right hand and shielded his eyes with his left even though he was wearing sunglasses. At 114 degrees Fahrenheit, the eyeballs become heat sensory organs.

Hank hustled away from the aircraft, his head down and his shirt-tail fluttering in the prop-wash. His body armor swayed back and forth on his torso, but he saw no point in tightening it this late in the game. Master Sergeant Aaron Chapman trotted alongside him, smiling as they stepped into the cool darkness of the passenger shed. After a young soldier checked their names against the manifest, Chapman pointed outside to an aluminum trailer that sold coffee.

Minutes later, away from the roar of jet engines and the heat of the airstrip, both men were sipping iced coffee from plastic cups labeled "Green Beans." They shared a moment of silence in the cool shade of a blast barrier and then walked toward the brigade headquarters. Hank glanced at the white-hot Iraqi sun and then at his watch. Less than forty-eight hours to go.

"Sir, it ain't been much fun, but it's been a real honor," Chapman said, his east Texas drawl a little thicker than usual.

Hank bumped his cup against Chapman's. "Likewise."

A few drops spilled into the brown talcum-powder dust and were swallowed as soon as they landed.

"You know, sir, I was thinking that we need to get the crew together one last time when we get back to Fort Bragg. Have something a little stronger than iced coffee, slap each other on the back, maybe tell some lies so the ladies will think we're heroes."

"Your idea sounds like a job for Lieutenant Upton. It's good professional development for a lieutenant to plan a social event."

"I'll bring some genuine Texas barbecue — *not* that soggy, vinegar-soaked pork butt you North Carolina folks call barbecue."

Hank shot him a glance, but Chapman smiled and continued. "I'm talking Black Angus beef brisket, smoked real slow over mesquite. And I'll bring a couple of cases of Lone Star—" Chapman began. His words were cut short by the blood-freezing wail of the warning siren. *Incoming.*

Hank and Chapman sprinted twenty meters to a bunker beside the path to headquarters. Hank dropped his iced coffee and gripped his M-4 with both hands as he ran. He flung himself into the bunker and Chapman followed a half second later, still holding his coffee, his hand wet with sticky caramel colored liquid.

"You move pretty fast, sir." Chapman panted as he shook the liquid off his hand.

"Thanks."

An incoming round sent a shiver through the bunker. Both men flinched, but neither stopped smiling.

"For a man your age, I mean."

"Your jokes were old ten months ago, Chapman. For a second, I thought about hitting the dirt, but the bunker was pretty close. That's a 107-millimeter rocket, by the way."

"Sure sounds like it. Probably firing from that spot by the canal southwest of the junkyard."

Another round struck south of them, much closer than the first. Chapman nodded as he sipped his coffee. "One-oh-sevens, for sure."

Another third round struck, this one even closer. A fourth exploded so close that dirt streamed from the sandbags on top of the bunker. Hank shifted to avoid the streams of falling dirt. He peered out the opening at the brigade headquarters and thanked God the headquarters building had a rebar-reinforced concrete roof.

"Headquarters' roof can take 107-millimeter rocket fire," Hank said.

"Yeah. But a 240 millimeter would punch right through."

"You suppose Abu Ghazali's boys have anything bigger than those one-oh-sevens?"

"Doubt it," Chapman answered. "I doubt it. Big IEDs are their specialty. But they got a resupply this week, according to that one report I showed you."

"I remember. That means they've got plenty of one-oh-sevens. God, don't let our brigade headquarters get hit this close to going home."

"God, don't let them get dirt in my coffee." Chapman laughed and curled himself over his cup to protect it. "You really going to retire when we get home, sir? You know you'll miss moments like this."

"I shall not miss the shrill, demented choirs of wailing shells," Hank said.

"Line of poetry?" Chapman asked.

Hank nodded and pressed himself into the corner of the bunker in anticipation that the next salvo of rockets would fall closer than the last. His heart pounded as he waited. *We are so close to going home.* Silence settled in. A minute later, Hank stood, his knees shaking.

"Four rounds and done, huh?" Chapman asked as he uncurled his torso and shoulders from around his coffee.

"Must not have been much of a resupply." Hank peered out at his plastic coffee cup, fifteen meters away, the coffee now nothing more than a damp patch under the merciless Iraqi sun.

"Shame about your coffee, sir." Chapman took a long sip and smacked his lips. "*Mine* sure is good."

"I *deserved* that coffee," Hank said as his empty paper cup danced away on the desert wind. Hank stood, poised just inside the bunker. Although he couldn't imagine why, Hank found the sight of his empty coffee cup disturbing. He found it even more disturbing that Abu Ghazali had the brass to launch rockets at the base after Hank had hunted him for three months.

Chapman grabbed Hank's sleeve. "Sir, let's stay here until we get the 'all clear,' then I'll buy you a replacement coffee."

"Why would Abu Ghazali's boys risk a broad daylight attack just to drop four rounds?"

"They're ranging us," Chapman said, "and they have plenty of rockets. Let's wait for the 'all clear.'"

"But they might need us in the headquarters."

"Play it safe. Let them handle—"

"There has been an indirect fire attack," a sultry female voice announced over the speaker system. Her words echoed over the base like the voice of a sports announcer at a game.

"I'm thinking I could have run to headquarters by now," Hank asked. "What are you thinking?"

"Me?" Chapman replied. "I'm just wondering if she's a redhead."

Hank stared across the open ground toward the headquarters building and then cast an anxious glance at the sky. "There are more rockets on the way."

"I know," Chapman said. "Now get back away from the opening, sir."

Hank stepped away from the bunker's opening. After fifteen months of combat, he trusted his intuition and so did Chapman. As if on cue, another round burst south of them, hitting a paved surface with a sharp crack. *God, please let them miss us all.*

They pressed into the farthest recesses of the bunker, their hands over their eyes and thumbs in their ears. A tight group of three rounds exploded in front of the headquarters building. The shock waves hit Hank like three vicious slaps to the chest and were followed by puffs of air like warm breaths. Neither man was smiling any longer. Two more rounds hit just north of the building, sending a spray of gravel and shrapnel buzzing around them. Hank squeezed his eyelids shut and felt the vibration in his teeth. Another round hit with a crack and a low rumble.

Hank shivered. Brigade headquarters had just taken a hit. Hank closed his eyes and thought of his wife. Chapman squirmed until he was tight against Hank's side, both men breathing harder now, both men knowing what was coming. Hank's mind conjured up images of his honeymoon in Costa Rica, of Sabine letting down her long chestnut hair under a tropical sun, of her silky skin, of her swimming beside him in turquoise waters. Seconds ticked by like fragments of eternity. Hank was wondering how Sabine would get by without him when the volley of rocket rounds struck, some so close that he saw the flash through his closed eyelids. The heat from the explosions burned away his visions of a tropical paradise and left him with a familiar thought. *Whatever happens next, I'll be reunited with my family back in Fayetteville, or with my sister Tracy in heaven.*

Minutes later, Hank's ears were still ringing, but he could discern the loudspeaker's sultry voice announce, "All clear." He and Chapman sprang from the bunker and sprinted to the brigade headquarters, where they nearly collided with three other soldiers. They all squeezed through the doorway but stopped in the entryway.

No lights. Power is still out. Thick dust hung in the air like an unspoken threat. One soldier coughed and turned to go, but Chapman put a hand on his shoulder and kept him in place.

"No smoke, just dust," Hank said. "The rocket didn't penetrate the ceiling."

Chapman fished a penlight from his pocket. "I got a light."

He sent a silver blade of light into the swirling brown air. Hank and the three soldiers followed him into the darkened building.

As the men crept forward, computers beeped, and distant voices echoed through the lightless corridors. Seconds later, the fluorescent lights buzzed and flickered, illuminating floors coated with dust and littered with chunks of concrete.

Chapman darted left into a small hallway, Hank close behind. The other soldiers continued straight. In the darkness, Hank and Chapman stumbled into a soldier who lay with his legs on the floor and his back against the wall.

"Tyson?" Hank shouted. "Is that you?" *God, please don't take him this close to going home.*

Chapman shone his penlight at the soldier, revealing squinting eyes and a shirt front spattered with blood.

Hank stepped over chunks of concrete and metal so he could kneel and grasp the man's shoulder. It was Specialist Tyson.

"Major McCaskill?" the injured soldier groaned.

"What happened?" Chapman asked as he knelt beside Hank. He handed Hank his penlight, opened his first aid pouch, and put on latex gloves.

"Sir, you won't believe this," Tyson answered, "but when that rocket hit the roof, a light fixture broke loose. Swung down and smacked me in the head."

Hank examined Tyson's arms, legs, and torso for additional injuries but found no other wounds. He held the penlight close to Tyson's scalp, revealing a jagged purple gash that oozed blood. Hank shone the penlight into Tyson's left eye and then his right. Both pupils narrowed in response. Hank switched the penlight off and then back on. He shone it into both of Tyson's eyes. Both pupils narrowed simultaneously. Hank nodded and smiled at Chapman, who smiled back.

Chapman eased Tyson's scalp apart, eliciting a groan and a few spurts of reddish-black blood. "Didn't penetrate your skull," Chapman remarked. "And you don't seem to have a concussion." He cleaned the wound with a sterile wipe, smeared Bacitracin on it, and then pressed gauze against it.

Hank glanced toward the Tactical Operations Center, the TOC, as the chatter of urgent voices and the crackle of radio transmissions echoed through the hallways.

"Go on ahead to the TOC, sir," Chapman said. "I got this."

Hank shook his head. "I'll stay until he's patched up." Hank moved the penlight to his mouth and applied pressure while Chapman wrapped Tyson's head in a crown of gauze.

"It's not as bad as it looks," Chapman said. "But it's a scalp wound, so you're bleeding like a stuck pig. You need to go to the clinic and get stitches when I'm done."

"Any other casualties?" Hank asked. He peered down the hallway, where patches of dust and fragments of concrete littered the floor.

"Not that I've seen," Tyson replied. "Thank God the roof held."

"Amen to that," Hank said.

Chapman leaned back and admired the bandage before tearing off his gloves. "Look at the bright side."

"What's that, sarge?"

"You'll get a purple heart out of this, and since it hit you in the head, we know it didn't damage anything vital."

"That's just plain wrong, Sergeant Chapman," Tyson said.

"All joking aside, can you walk?" Hank asked.

"Yes sir. Well enough to get to the clinic."

Hank helped Tyson to his feet and put an arm around his shoulders to make sure his first few steps were steady while Chapman repacked the first aid kit.

"Keep pressure on that bandage, tough guy," Chapman yelled as Tyson turned the corner.

"Aaron," Hank said, "go check in with the Coneheads. Make sure those guys are keyed on Abu Ghazali. I'll go check the office. See if our team took any casualties."

"Sir," Chapman said with a grin, "those guys are signals intelligence professionals. They would be offended to know you call them 'Coneheads.'"

"So, don't let the SIGINT professionals *know* I call them Cone-heads."

"Yes, sir," Chapman said, "but I think they know."

"I'll go see if any of our guys got hit."

2

Hank trotted through the dusty hallways toward the TOC and stopped at the door to the intelligence section. He took a deep breath and opened it, knowing he might see some of his soldiers with serious injuries. To his surprise, his three day shift analysts – Litton, Decker, and Davis – were at their workstations, plugging away on their computers. In happier moments, Hank sometimes called them "Larry, Darrell, and Darrell, but he wouldn't call them that now. His deputy, Lieutenant Upton, stood by the wall map, oblivious to Hank's presence as he traced a line along an irrigation canal with his finger. Hank exhaled heavily and looked through the intelligence office and into the TOC. When he saw no signs of injuries among any of the brigade's soldiers, he uttered a silent prayer of thanks. Hank then took comfort in the cacophony of fingers clattering on keyboards and voices squawking from radios. That meant the TOC was operational.

Decker, a tall, bookish man with red hair, was searching through reports of weapons caches nearby, his eyes wide and his glasses reflecting the flickering green of the photographs he scanned through. Litton was closest to Hank, his broad shoulders and thick chest rocking to a private rhythm. He grimaced as he hammered away on his laptop, earbuds jammed into his ears, his shaved head bobbing to the sounds of rapid-fire guitar chords and guttural screaming.

Hank looked through the open doorway of the intelligence office and into the TOC, where Davis was drumming on his keyboard too, but in a slower rhythm. Davis's clean-cut good looks, precise haircut, and strong chin contrasted with the white scars that decorated the dark brown skin of his knuckles. None of his intelligence analysts looked like intelligence analysts, Hank thought. Decker looked like a professor, Litton looked like a biker, and Davis looked like a cop. Davis had pulled up video feed from a tower-mounted CCTV camera pointed in the direction the rockets had come from.

Just then, Lieutenant Upton noticed Hank and turned from the map. He smiled like someone to whom rocket attacks were as commonplace as bad weather. "Welcome back from Baghdad, sir," he said in a soft Virginia accent. "How was it?"

"Lovely this time of year," Hank said, looking up at Upton, who stood at least five inches taller than him. "Any casualties?"

"We took a couple of rockets, but no casualties in the TOC," Upton said with a smile. Then his tone changed. "I expect we have a couple around the brigade area this time. S-1 is getting a casualty count right now. We're supporting response options."

"Where is the new team of intel analysts?"

"Inbound." Upton said. "They take over in three hours."

"I hope they don't come in early. I want our team to bag Abu Ghazali."

"You think Abu Ghazali was behind the rocket attacks?"

"No doubt," Hank said. "What are y'all working on?"

Upton pointed to a spot on the map. "We're analyzing the terrain around the likely point of origin. Like I said, ops is working on a response already."

"That's good, but we've all studied that terrain until our eyeballs hurt, so you can stop. Abu Ghazali knows our brigade is leaving. Those rockets were his parting shot."

"I don't know, sir," Upton said, his soft Virginia accent conveying uncertainty.

Hank gestured at the map. "That launch point is consistent with what Chapman and I heard from the bunker. Good work. Now, get Decker and Litton to focus on Abu Ghazali and his boys. Then have Davis find out what air assets we have nearby that might help us confirm Abu Ghazali's presence."

"On it, sir."

Hank grabbed Litton's massive left shoulder and motioned for him to remove his earbuds.

"What ya need, sir?"

"First, turn your music down so you don't go deaf by age thirty. Second, if you want screaming guitars, put on some Thin Lizzy."

Litton chuckled. "My Dad used to say the same thing." He turned the volume down after putting the earbuds back in.

Hank shook his head and walked to the map with lieutenant Upton. After studying the map, Hank stepped into the TOC, unslung his M-4, and secured it in a weapons rack. Then he picked up his M-9 Beretta pistol, checked the chamber, strapped on a thigh holster, and shoved the pistol into it until it locked into place.

He looked around the TOC as he poured himself a cup of coffee. A dozen soldiers sat at their computers; their keystrokes nearly harmonized as they whispered into their headset microphones. Another two were arranging unit markers on a wall-sized map. The operations officer, Captain Russo, stood above the fray like a conductor, somehow balancing a radio mic in his left hand, a pen in his right, and a secure telephone between his chin and left shoulder. A large screen in the center of the room displayed information about current operations in a grid. He frowned. *We should have Predator feed on the big screen.* He watched as a map of the base took the place of the information grid. A soldier was plotting red dots on the locations where the rockets had hit. Hank sipped his lukewarm coffee. *Hmm. Turpentine, with undertones of mud and subtle hints of cigarette ash.*

"Sir," Upton called out. "Come look at this."

Hank took another sip, then tossed his coffee in the trash. He walked back into the intelligence office, where Upton and Litton stood beside the map. Upton handed him a paper.

"This report is two weeks old," Upton said. "A source of undetermined reliability claimed that Abu Ghazali would personally supervise a rocket attack once he got that resupply."

Hank read the report and looked at the map. "If that report is accurate, Abu Ghazali is probably at the launch site." Then he shouted into the TOC, "Davis! Why don't we have Predator feed?"

"No UAVs in the area," Davis replied.

Hank muttered and walked back into the TOC. Captain Russo still held the secure telephone under his chin, but was speaking into the radio mic. He paused long enough to mouth instructions to the soldier who controlled the video showing on the big screen.

"Russo's got his hands full, literally," Hank said to Upton. "Get with Davis. There are no Predators in the immediate area. Have him find one that's homeward bound. Try to buy, borrow, or steal some camera time. Do whatever it takes."

"Wilco."

Hank returned to Litton's workstation and skimmed a few dozen reports. "Three of the most recent reports mentioned the word 'motorbike.'"

Litton removed his earbuds. "I noticed, sir."

"That means he was probably on site, but he's mobile and nearly anonymous. We have to act *now*." When Hank looked up from the reports, he saw Upton in front of the map again. Hank joined him.

"What you got, Upton?"

Upton grinned. "I cut a deal. We'll borrow time on Predator coming back from Samarra. It's low on gas, but it's ours. Davis's chatting with the payload operator."

"What are we doing for them in return?" Hank asked.

"I told them we had a hot lead on Abu Ghazali."

"And?"

"I said I'd inform General Simpson that their support was critical in bagging him."

"You're a class act, Upton."

"Thank you, sir."

"Now, let's hope my hunch is right."

"I wouldn't sweat it," Upton replied. "I've got Decker cross-checking recent reports for names of suspected associates of Abu Ghazali."

Davis yelled from the TOC, "Major McCaskill, sir! Captain Russo is off the phone."

Hank stepped back into the TOC and faced Captain Russo, who reported, "Third battalion has two patrols in the area. We'll know something in a couple of minutes."

Before Hank could respond, Chapman bustled into the S-2 office, wearing a mischievous grin. "Sir, I just gave the Coneheads an attitude adjustment."

"And?"

"They haven't had a hit on Abu Ghazali's cell phone in four days."

"You serious?"

"As a heart attack," Chapman answered.

"Then why are you smiling?" Hank asked.

"Abu personally supervised a rocket attack against Taji about two months ago. Remember?"

"Yes," Hank said. "One rocket hit a barrier and sent concrete fragments through the barber shop. Injured one barber and two soldiers."

"Abu Ghazali's cell phone was silent for about four days before that attack and about two days after."

"So, he's not using his cell phone. Do the Coneheads have anything on walkie-talkie comms in the area near the point of origin?"

Chapman's eyes lit up. "Funny you should ask. They just picked up a lot of radio chatter around the point of origin and some more around a nearby town. The sanitized report should hit Litton's workstation in about a minute."

Hank leaned in close to the map. "You got a location?"

"It's in the report," Chapman said.

"Yes!" Hank shouted.

Hank, Upton, and Chapman stood poised by the map for ninety long seconds. When the report came in, Litton called out the coordinates while Upton plotted the location on the map.

"It's a big ellipse," Upton said as he drew a broad oval on the map with a watercolor marker. "However, we can rule out most of the real estate inside it."

"Double-checking the report," Litton called out. "The language they used indicated they were talking about rockets. And the transmission times coincide with the launch times."

"Roger," Upton acknowledged.

"He won't be anywhere east of this canal," Hank said, tracing another irrigation canal southwest of the base. "And he won't be anywhere west of this other canal right here. There's a palm grove half a click from the center of the ellipse. Decker could you—?"

"Even as we speak, sir," Decker said, "I am pulling up previous reporting on that location."

"I *know* that palm grove and that cluster of buildings," Hank said, jabbing his index finger at the map. "There's a garage beside that walled compound, right about here. They do auto repairs."

Upton grinned. "I suspect they also do rocket storage."

Hank nodded. "As I recall, a patrol checked it out two months ago, but didn't find anything conclusive. Decker, you got a history on that garage?" Decker's fingers drummed on the keyboard.

"I have something far better, gentlemen," Decker responded. "That garage belongs to a suspected associate of Abu Ghazali named Tariq Albakir al Douri."

Hank nodded. "With any luck, we just might bag Abu Ghazali this time."

"Assuming he's still there," Upton said. Hank shot him a sharp glance.

"I'll go feed Tariq al Douri's name back to the Coneheads," Chapman said. "See what they got."

Hank felt a spark of hope. "Come on, Predator," he said, as if encouraging it. "We still have time to bag a bad guy."

"Oh yeah!" Litton shouted. "We just picked up more radio chatter at the garage."

"Yes!" Hank shouted. "He's still there. Davis, let us know as soon as we've got Predator feed."

"Be patient, sir," Davis replied, his voice conveying enthusiasm. "We'll get him this time. Also, sir, captain Russo said that one of third battalion's patrols is near enough to roll on Abu Ghazali."

"Good work, Davis," Hank said before whispering, "Come on Predator."

Forty minutes later, Hank stood in the TOC, watching the video feed from the Predator on the big screen. The current view showed a deserted Iraqi road near the supposed location of Abu Ghazali.

"Sir," Lieutenant Upton said as he tapped Hank's shoulder. "What did the guys at Corps G-2 say about your assessment of Abu Ghazali?"

Hank turned and tilted his head back to face Upton. "They're still hung up on his affiliations. Agency rep says he's Al Qaeda. Corps G-2 says he's Ansar al Islam. Coneheads say he's a little fish and we shouldn't worry about him. Brits claim he's a Saudi who went to Afghanistan to fight but had a disagreement with Bin Laden, so he's not really Al Qaeda. Canadians claim he's originally Paki and has ties to Haqqani, but that's based on single-source HUMINT." Hank turned back toward the wall map. "None of which matters. We need to know *where* he is, not *who* he is. I don't care about his life story. I just want him dead."

Lieutenant Colonel Brian Etheridge, the brigade executive officer, gestured for Hank to come stand beside him in the center of the TOC.

Hank went to stand by Brian's side. Around them, a dozen soldiers peered into computer monitors, their faces drawn tight and illuminated by the pale blue of their screens. A tense silence had settled over the TOC, broken only by terse whispers, off-key bursts of radio chatter, and the dissonant rhythm of fingers on keyboards.

"So, the Old Man's gonna let you run this one?" Hank asked.

"Yeah," Brian said. "But third battalion has the football. We're just in overwatch. The old man is on the phone with General Simpson."

"Sir," Litton whispered from around the corner, "we just got more radio chatter. Don't have internals yet, but the location matches."

Hank nodded and looked back at the screen. The Predator's cameras now transmitted images of a typical Iraqi compound. Tall palms towered over bushy orange trees and a cluster of brown concrete buildings. Pools of shadow and light rippled across the ground as the wind stirred the palm fronds. The compound overlooked wheat fields, a small junkyard, and an unkempt patch of ground that used to be a vineyard. Six Humvees prowled toward the edge of the grove, their fifty-caliber Browning machine guns and grenade launchers ready.

A dismounted platoon of thirty-two infantrymen walked alongside the Humvees in two columns, their weapons pointed outward. The columns slowed as they snaked into the grove. Another platoon established a perimeter around the compound as two Apache helicopter flew low and fast overhead. Even Abu Ghazali would have a hard time escaping this trap.

As he watched, the dismounted platoon halted about eighty meters from the garage and set up an inner perimeter. One squad approached the garage in a wedge formation behind the lead Humvee. A man clad in civilian clothes and body armor, obviously an interpreter, followed the soldiers.

The lead Humvee accelerated toward the door of the garage and then skidded to a halt. Two soldiers jumped from the rear doors and went to the front of the Humvee. There they attached chains to the garage door and stepped aside as the Humvee crawled in reverse. As the chains grew taut, a distorted radio call rattled through the speaker, the only discernible part of which was "second platoon taking fire."

Rifle muzzles flashed from behind the charred carcass of an abandoned pickup truck. The soldiers returned fire, their bullets tearing through the palm grove and sending chunks of wood and metal flying. Two figures emerged from behind the truck and ran eastward, but rifle fire cut them down within seconds. Fifteen months earlier, the soldiers in the TOC would have cheered, but after fifteen months of almost constant combat, they remained silent. None of the soldiers wanted to look at the bodies of the two insurgents.

Something about this doesn't look right, Hank thought. As the video closed in on the enemy dead, Brian shouted, "Shift view, back to the garage!"

Davis's fingers hammered his keyboard, and a moment later, the view shifted to show the Humvee dragging the garage doors away and raising a cloud of dust. A squad of soldiers ran through the dust cloud and disappeared inside. *Please, God, no booby traps this time.*

As Hank watched the garage on the screen, a motorbike darted across the top of the screen, speeding northward toward the perimeter, and raising a dust plume.

"We've got a rabbit," the operations officer announced.

"On it, sir," a soldier replied. A few seconds later, a distorted radio transmission came in. "This is Gunslinger Two. One rabbit on a motorbike, moving northwest toward MSR Tampa."

The Predator's camera swiveled to follow the man on the motorbike, and Hank know immediately that the outer perimeter might not catch him.

"Keep the Predator feed on the garage!" Brian said. "We've got a perimeter and we've got Apaches overhead. Captain Russo, check in with the adjacent battalion to the north."

"Could have been him," Hank whispered.

Brian nodded. "Let's hope the outer perimeter catches him."

Seconds later, a radio call announced that the motorbike had slipped through the perimeter.

"Not again," Upton groaned.

"Upton," Hank said over his shoulder, "have our guys plot time phase lines on the major roads. Use a base speed of 50 clicks. I want to know the farthest he could travel in ten-minute increments. We still may catch him."

Hank and Brian watched the screen as the soldiers emptied the garage, box by box. Both men cursed under their breath when it became obvious the only items in the garage were car parts and toolboxes.

"This is the place," Hank said. "Did you see the scorch marks by the junkyard?"

Brian nodded.

Movement outside the compound walls caught Hank's attention. Two soldiers were pulling a man out of a spider hole behind the garage. Hank smiled as they pulled a second man from the hole. Other soldiers separated the two men, zip-tied them, and photographed their faces. The interpreter and two other soldiers shoved them to the ground between the lead Humvee and the garage where they would be safe from rifle fire.

Brian smiled. "Now we're getting somewhere."

"Maybe one of them is our boy," Hank said.

A few minutes later, Upton asked Hank to step back into the S-2 office. Hank walked over to Decker's computer and joined Upton, Chapman, and Litton in a huddle around a large computer screen.

"Gentlemen," Decker announced. "The photograph on the left is our file photo of Abu Ghazali. The photo on the right is detainee one."

"Not the same man," Upton said.

"Clearly, sir. Not him"

"What about his buddy?" Chapman asked.

Decker typed, and the photo on the right changed. "We are now looking at detainee two."

"That's not him either," Chapman said before kicking the desk.

"I'll go break the news to Lieutenant Colonel Etheridge."

When Hank returned to the TOC, Brian watched him closely. Hank shook his head and whispered, "not him."

Brian nodded but kept a poker face. They wouldn't tell the soldiers just yet.

A radio call came in, informing them that one detainee had admitted knowing Tariq Albakir al Douri. A second radio call came in, telling them the Predator would be going off station in five minutes due to low fuel. Brian started to say something when a third radio call came in.

"This is Gunslinger Two. We have troops in contact west of Taji. Breaking station to support troops in contact. Motorbike last seen heading north on MSR Tampa in heavy traffic."

The operations officer acknowledged and turned to Brian. "Sir, we lost him."

"Roger. Our Predator is out of gas and our Apache is going off station to support troops in contact west of Taji."

"Let's see what we can make of the Apache's gun camera footage," Hank said. "We won't have it for at least an hour after they land, but if we can tease out the license plate number, we may get him."

Brian shook his head. "I wouldn't hold my breath. Plate's probably stolen. We'll be on a plane by the time the Iraqis find the tag's owner."

Something else still gnawed at Hank, something about the two men who had fled the compound.

"Brian, the two men who were killed were running southeast, right?"

"Yeah."

"If they wanted to fight, why didn't they stay and fight? Why did they fire first instead of just running?"

"Beats me."

"Davis, how much time do we have left on the Predator?" Hank asked.

"Just over three minutes, sir."

"What if those two were ordered to flee and take a parting shot as they went? What if they were a deliberate misdirection?"

"I think I follow you," Brian said.

"Davis," Hank said, "get the sensor operator to pan back to the southwest of the compound!"

"What are we looking for?"

"The presence of the abnormal or the absence of the normal," Hank answered.

The video feed focused on a sandy area southwest of the compound and panned about, revealing a vacant patch of ground.

"I don't see anything but a footpath," Brian said.

"Exactly," Hank said. "A footpath to where? There's no outhouse, no burn pit, no dirt patch where somebody parked a car. Nothing. How much time we got left, Davis?"

"Three minutes."

"Try to zoom in on the spot where the footpath ends. What do you see?"

"Just trash."

"Close in on that piece of trash there," Hank said, shining his laser pointer at the screen. The view zoomed in on a small triangle-shaped rag.

"Captain Russo," Brian said, "get third battalion to check it out."

Moments later, a squad of soldiers tiptoed toward the triangle-shaped rag. One soldier moved ahead of the others to check for booby traps. A tense silence settled on the TOC as the soldier tugged the rag. It didn't move.

That's not a rag. That's the corner of a buried tarpaulin.

The squad checked the area again for booby traps, and then two soldiers pulled the tarpaulin back. A square wooden hatch lay beneath it.

"Jackpot," Hank said.

Several soldiers cheered just before the Predator broke station to return to base. The video changed to show the underside of the Predator's tail.

Brian and Hank listened as radio reports confirmed that a staircase under the hatch led to an underground room. A moment later, another radio report confirmed that the room held at least a dozen boxes of rockets, stacks of mortar shells, and a crate of garage door openers.

"Well, I guess we found Abu Ghazali's stash of IED components and one-oh-sevens," Hank said.

"One of his stashes, anyway," Brian said. "Nice work."

"Thanks, but Upton and my analysts did the hard part."

Brian looked around the TOC and announced, "Listen up." The soldiers turned from their computer screens and map boards to listen. "You all performed well and honorably this afternoon. I am proud to have served with every one of you, and I'd do it again. We had one last shot at Abu Ghazali, and we took it. We did our best, but sometimes the bad guy gets away. On the other hand, we put a serious dent in their supply chain. The Old Man is going to be proud."

Brian turned to face Hank and continued. "Speaking of the Old Man, he wants to see you at 1700, right after that new team of intel analysts takes over."

"About what?" Hank asked.

"You know what it's about."

"My mind is made up."

"Right," Brian chuckled.

"Colonel Spelman won't change it."

3

A few minutes before 1700, Hank wound through the narrow corridors of the brigade headquarters building, suppressing the urge to sneeze. He reached Brian's office, looked up at the placard that read, "Executive Officer," and cleared his throat.

Brian looked up from his desk. "Catch any bad guys today?"

"No," Hank replied, "but let me tell you about the one that got away."

"I already know that story. Anyway, the Old Man is ready to see you."

"The 'Old Man' is younger than me," Hank responded. "You sure he's ready?"

"He is. The question is, are *you* ready?"

Hank stepped past Brian's office and knocked on the doorframe of Colonel Spelman's office.

From inside, Spelman said, "Enter."

Hank stepped inside to find the colonel talking on the telephone while a soldier boxed up papers stacked beside the desk. Spelman looked up with a grin and covered the phone's mouthpiece with a sinewy right hand that sported a gold and sapphire West Point ring.

"Almost done," he said to Hank before uncovering the phone's mouthpiece and resuming his conversation.

Hank waited about a minute before Spelman hung up the phone and stood. He was a little taller than Hank, and a little younger. Except for the streaks of silver at his temples, he looked like a triathlete in his late thirties.

"Good afternoon, Major McCaskill. I want to talk to you about something, but not here. Let's take a walk."

The two men stepped out into the sweltering Iraqi afternoon. Pigeons cooed in the tree overhead, barely audible over the sound of a jet engine warming up on the airstrip. Hank's eyes drifted to two fresh craters that lay between them and the airfield. An EOD team had already measured the craters and marked them with wooden stakes and rope.

Spelman pulled a large cigar from his cargo pocket. "Now, this here," he said, admiring it, "is a genuine Cuban Cohiba. I bought a box of these from a cigar shop in Baghdad last month. Customs won't let me take them home, so we might as well smoke 'em while we got 'em."

Spelman handed Hank a cigar and stopped walking. Hank sniffed at the label of his cigar, nodded, and put it in his pocket. He looked around and made a mental note of the nearest bunker.

"I'll smoke mine later, sir," Hank said, waving away Colonel Spelman's offer of a light. Spelman started walking again.

"Hank," Spelman said, pausing to light up, "this brigade has performed well in combat. We rolled up a couple hundred bad guys, pacified an area the size of New Hampshire, and we killed dozens of IED teams. We didn't lose a single soldier. General Simpson was very pleased when I told him some of Abu Ghazali's IED teams were killing each other because they thought one of their own had ratted them out."

"I'm just glad to be going home with all of our boys and girls alive,"

Hank responded. "And I wish we could have taken down Abu Ghazali along with the guys placing the IEDs."

"We did well, Hank, and you know it."

"We did, but every day I wish Reyes and Ahrens hadn't gotten hit."

"Sergeant Reyes lost his legs but kept his life."

"Reyes didn't lose his legs, sir. Abu Ghazali took them."

Colonel Spelman frowned. "You and Brian are solid officers, but you two should stop taking it personally every time Abu Ghazali's boys launch an attack. As for Ahrens, he's one tough soldier. Did you know he wants to stay in? Even with a prosthetic leg. I told him I'd write him a recommendation."

"I heard Reyes opted for medical retirement, sir."

"Yeah, Hank, that's what he wanted."

"Sir, every night I go to bed wondering if we missed some little thing that would have led us to Abu Ghazali."

"Old Abu is on the run, thanks in part to you. And probably changing his pants after this afternoon's raid."

Hank's gut churned at the thought that Abu Ghazali had slipped through his fingers again. Iraq – and indeed the world – would not know peace as long as men like Abu Ghazali had a free hand. Hank knew what Abu Ghazali was capable of, and he didn't want Abu on the run and afraid. Hank wanted him stone-cold dead. Instead of telling Colonel Spelman all this, however, Hank just ground his teeth and said, "I feel like I let my men down by not catching him."

"You didn't. You just feel that way because you're a perfectionist. You're also a leader with a strong moral compass. And the Army needs good leaders."

"Sir, I know where you're going with this. The thing is, I already have an approved retirement date. My die has been cast."

"Your die has been cast, huh? You're a soldier!"

"That's true today, but in a few weeks I'll be a civilian."

"The Army's in your blood," Spelman said, pointing his cigar at Hank for emphasis. "You'd bleed green if I cut you. What on earth are you going to do after you retire? Take your wife on Napa Valley wine tours? Drink expensive coffee and work crossword puzzles? You'll die of boredom."

Hank stopped walking and gazed thoughtfully across the airfield. Spelman stopped and blew a smoke ring into the hot air. Hank watched it dissipate.

"I plan to grow tomatoes."

"Excuse me?" Spelman laughed. "Grow tomatoes?"

"Yes, sir. Tomatoes. Sabine and I have a house down by the Cape Fear River. It's not out in the country, but it has a big back yard, and it backs up to the woods. Except for one tour in Germany, that's where we've lived since we got married. Or rather that's where she and the boys have lived. I was gone a lot." He recalled the sound of their three sons playing on the swing set and the trampoline in the back yard. Of course, on most days, a half dozen other kids from the neighborhood would be there too. Hank imagined their laughter now, even over the roar of jet engines.

"Go on," Spelman said, once again gesturing with his cigar.

"As I was saying, sir, that house is my home. But since 2001, I haven't spent much time there. It's been constant deployments, and when we weren't deploying, we were recovering from deployment, getting ready to deploy, or training other units to deploy. I understand we're an army at war, but nearly forty percent of military intelligence officers have *never* deployed to combat. It's the same guys deploying again and again. I am on the traveling team, and I'm tired. I'm done with war."

"You don't seem to have much of a career plan. Look, with the work you've done as my intel chief, you're on track to make lieutenant colonel next year. And then you'll be up for a battalion command. After that, who knows? Division G-2? Maybe higher if you play your cards right."

"Sir, I'm a forty-nine-year-old major. And Sabine doesn't want a husband who wears a colonel's rank. She just wants a husband who will be home at night. And I just want to live out my days at peace with my fellow man."

"A noble sentiment. And one that you're not made to live out."

"Sabine is a nurse. Right now, she's working part-time, but she can get more hours if we need additional income. Add in my retirement check, and we can live comfortably."

"You might change your mind once you realize how hard it is to 'live comfortably' on what you'll be making. Besides, you need more than money. I've seen guys like you retire, guys who don't realize how much they liked being a soldier until they're wearing civilian clothes."

"Sir, I was a teacher for the four years I was out of the army. I could teach again. But before I decide anything, I'm going to take a year off and grow tomatoes."

"Hank, if you want to teach, stay in, come work for me. My Academy roommate runs the schoolhouse at Fort Leavenworth and I'm going there for my next assignment. We can hook you up with a teaching job. The Army needs officers like you, officers who can teach."

"Sir, the army always needs officers like me until one day when, all of a sudden, it doesn't. Besides, my wife needs me. Not *a man like me*, but *me*. Do you know this is my fifth combat deployment to the Middle East? Did you know that nearly half of all intelligence majors have never deployed, guys like me have permanent slots on the traveling team?"

"Of course, I know all that. I also know that retirement can crush a man like you."

"Sir, you know the kind of things Abu Ghazali did. I took my shot at him and I missed. I'm sorry I let you down, but I've seen enough war. Sometimes the good guy gets tired, and sometimes the bad guy gets away."

"You've seen enough, huh?" Spelman said, pausing to draw on his cigar. "Only the dead have seen the end of war."

"Santayana," Hank said. "Although it's often attributed to Plato. Regardless of who said it, this old major needs a rest."

Spelman exhaled a plume of cigar smoke. "We all need a rest."

"I'm glad you understand, sir."

Spelman stopped walking. "Look, Hank, I know you're older than other majors, and I know you're an odd duck."

"I prefer to think of myself as 'eccentric,' sir."

"Whatever," Spelman said. He tossed his cigar into the dust. "If you don't want to do what's best for the army, you should at least do what's best for your family." Spelman ground the cigar to a pulp with his boot while looking into Hank's eyes.

Hank smiled. "Have you ever tasted my homegrown tomatoes, sir?"

Spelman did not return Hank's smile. "No, I haven't. We'll talk again soon. In the meantime, think about what I said. You haven't seen the end of war."

4

Fayetteville, North Carolina
October 10, 2008

Ballinger looked up from his desk as Detective Agosto sauntered through the maze of cubicles in the station's third floor, nursing a cup of coffee, and flexing his shoulder muscles, making them bulge against his shirt. Agosto stopped in front of Ballinger's cubicle as if he had noticed something hanging on the wall.

"What is it, Gus?" Ballinger asked.

Agosto smiled and pointed to an award that hung on the wall beside Ballinger. His hand trembled. "Boss, we got a problem."

"What kind of problem?"

Agosto leaned in close and lowered his voice. "That kid we been looking out for, Candyman."

"Yeah?" Ballinger said, his pen still scrawling across paper.

"Just got picked up for possession. It's only marijuana this time, but he had over a dime bag, so it's more serious than last time."

Ballinger stopped writing and looked up.

"Stupid kid also had a switchblade in his back pocket," Agosto said. "And with his record ... ."

Ballinger squeezed the pen in his hand so hard that it crackled. "Where is he now?"

"Murray's processing him," Agosto said as he drained the contents of his cup. "He's cooperating."

Ballinger gulped. "Has he asked for either of us yet?"

"No, but he will."

"Murray's smart, and Candyman ... well, he's not exactly a genius. Murray may ask him about Voodoo before the kid asks for us."

"Yep. That's why I wanted to let you know, boss."

"Thing is," Ballinger said, "I've already told that kid I couldn't help him if he got picked up again."

"Situation's changed since you told him that."

"Yes, it has. But I can't just make the charge go away if Murray's on it. That man's bucking to make detective. He won't play."

An hour later, Ballinger grabbed two fistfuls of Candyman's baggy football jersey and shoved him through the door to the back stairwell.

Candyman tried to twist away, but Ballinger held him fast. "Yo, you ain't got to be so rough, Detective."

"Shut your pie-hole, son," Ballinger responded before he dragged the young man down three flights of stairs. At the ground floor, he fished a key from his pocket and turned off the alarm on an emergency exit. He opened the door and shoved Candyman into a litter-strewn alley behind the station. Agosto was waiting nearby in a dark blue Crown Vic. Before Candyman could straighten his jersey, Ballinger frog-marched him all the way to the car's open back door.

"Come on, DB," Candyman said. "Let up on me, man."

Agosto sat in the driver's seat, tapping his fingers on the wheel. Ballinger pushed Candyman into the back seat and settled himself in the front passenger seat. He turned to Candyman as the car sped away.

"Where we going?" Candyman asked.

"Far, far away," Ballinger said. "You got an uncle in South Carolina, right?"

"Yeah," Candyman said.

"He told you that you could come live with him, right?"

"Hey, I don't want to—"

"Shut up, son!" Ballinger snapped. "We're taking you to the bus station. You're gonna buy a ticket to Columbia."

Candyman smiled at Agosto. "Yo, Detective Agosto, is this how you treat—"

"Shut up and listen," Agosto said.

"Give me your uncle's phone number," Ballinger said. "I'll call him and tell him you're on your way. He should be there waiting for you. If he's not, call me immediately. And don't talk to other people on the bus. Pretend to be sleeping."

"I need to go get my stuff from my grandmother's house," Candyman said.

Ballinger reached into his coat pocket and pulled out a pair of hundred-dollar bills.

"Buy some new clothes - ones that don't sag. I'll send your uncle some money in a few days and he can take you to Wal-Mart."

Candyman scoffed at the bills. "Wal-Mart? A man like me needs some *style*. I figure at least five hundred for a new wardrobe. Shoes alone gonna cost a hundred. You feel me?"

"Candyman!" Agosto yelled, causing Candyman to sit up straight and stop talking.

"Okay, Detective Agosto," Candyman said. "You got my attention."

"You are going to wind up dead if you don't follow instructions this time. You feel *me*?"

"Y'all are serious about this, huh? What's going on? All I did was sell some weed."

Ballinger looked back at Candyman and shook his head. "You are in over your head, son. Way over."

"I think I know what this is about. It's that guy that I set up for y'all a few weeks back, isn't it. He's your boy now, ain't he?"

"You're a loose end," Agosto said. "The big fish don't like loose ends. You had a chance to lay low, and you blew it. We're giving you a second chance."

Candyman took the bills between his index finger and thumb and looked at Ballinger. "Right. Catch a bus to Columbia. Stay with my uncle a while. I got this. But you gotta spot me at least another hundred."

Ballinger shook his head as Agosto stopped the car in front of the bus station. "For God's sake, lay low young man. For real this time."

5

Chapel Hill, North Carolina
October 13, 2008

Iqbal Orakzai crept into his apartment and eased the door shut even though the wind tried to tug the doorknob from his grasp. He moved slowly, his brown eyes darting around, and slender frame padding across the floor like a cat. He glanced toward the bedroom where his roommate slept and exhaled deeply. After easing his book bag onto the sofa, he drank a glass of milk. Then he went to his room, undressed, and lay down. Iqbal had just closed his eyes when his roommate Bilal spoke to him from the other side of the bedroom door.

"Iqbal, did I tell you that my father called today?"

"No," Iqbal said, turning to lie on his left side, facing the door. "Why do you speak to me when I'm trying to sleep?"

"Because that's when my words will sink in. My father asked me if I had seen my mother since my trip to Lahore last summer."

"It's good that you are speaking to your father again."

"Not really. Anyway, I told him I had heard from her last month. Then we argued, as we always do."

Iqbal said nothing.

"Don't you want to know why we argued?" Bilal asked.

Iqbal sighed. "All right. Tell me why you argued this time."

"I said he has it all wrong. I told him our home country does not need *land* reform. Our home country needs *spiritual* reform."

"Why do you correct your father?" Iqbal asked. "That is not your place. You should respect him. He has devoted much of his life to land reform."

"Actually, he tried to correct *me*," Bilal replied with a chuckle, "and that is what started the argument. He said that America is our home country now, and that Pakistan is our past. Land reform is the only way forward, according to him. He said, 'Fundamentalism is but a pit along the road from feudalism to modernity.'"

"And you disagreed with him?"

"Of course. But what really set him off was that I told him Mother's new husband is a devout Muslim who, unlike him, takes matters of God quite seriously."

"That's all very interesting, Bilal," Iqbal groaned, "but right now I am more interested in sleep than in your disagreements with your father. I have a hard day ahead of me tomorrow and an exam on Friday. I need to rest."

"Yes. You need to rest. I'll ask you the same thing I asked my father: How can you rest when America is killing Muslims all over the world?"

"Humans of *all* faiths are killing other humans all over the world, Bilal, and they have been since Cain killed Abel. It is what we call *history*."

"Yes, yes, history. Anyway, tomorrow night I am going to meet with a real Muslim."

"The crazy man you met at CrossFit?"

"He is not crazy," Bilal laughed. "In fact, he makes perfect sense if you listen to him. He promised to train me how to use his guns. You should come with me."

"No thank you, Bilal. A dentist has little need for guns."

"Just go with me this once, so I don't have to go alone."

"I don't think so, Bilal. Good night."

"If your father were still alive, what would he think of you, Iqbal? What if he knew that you value your sleep more than you value Muslim lives?"

"Good night, Bilal," Iqbal said, slapping his pillow as he rolled onto his right side again. Iqbal lay on his side, staring at the wall in front of him, where the shadows of tree branches swayed back and forth like fingers tugging at the wallpaper.

6

After a layover in Kuwait City and delays involving Turkish airspace, a brief stopover in Germany, and a bumpy ride across the Atlantic, Hank sat upright on the C-17, his heart pounding as the plane's engines whined to a stop. By his watch, it had been forty-eight hours since his unit had left Balad.

When the aircrew announced they were on American soil, Hank added his voice to the cheer that erupted from the passengers. Outside, it was mid-morning, but to Hank time was no longer measured in hours or days, time was now measured in the number of heartbeats until he found himself in Sabine's arms.

He waddled off the C-17 beneath the weight of his gear and joined the other soldiers as they assembled in a loose formation. They shed their gear quickly and loaded it onto four cargo trucks. The brigade sergeant major then marched them toward an aircraft hangar that hummed with the murmurs of waiting families. Hank held his head high and his face straight ahead, but his eyes darted around the hangar looking for Sabine as the formation entered.

Bleachers lined three sides of the hangar, filled with wives and children who could no longer resist the urge to stand. Most of the soldiers tried to look for their families discreetly, but a few smiled and looked around, and one even waved. At last, the Sergeant Major called the formation to a halt and gave them a "left face" command so that they faced a podium in the center of the hangar. Hank still did not see Sabine.

General Briggs stepped up to the lectern, his broad, uniformed chest bristling with medals and his craggy face glowing with genuine joy. He looked around the hangar and smiled in approval.

"On behalf of a grateful nation," he began, gripping the lectern as if it were the wheel of a ship, "I'd like to say welcome home, warriors." The soldiers cheered until General Briggs cleared his throat. "Colonel Spelman, you and the brave men and women of this brigade have borne the burden of freedom. You have taken the fight to the enemy, felt the satisfaction of victory, and suffered the sting of sacrifice. And today, you know the joy of homecoming." General Briggs continued, thanking the soldiers and their families for their service. Hank stood in a daze, not listening, not because he didn't care, but because this was the fifth time he had been through this ritual. He ached for the moment he would hold Sabine again. *General Briggs is a good man and one of the Army's best leaders,* Hank thought. *I should listen to him.* He turned his attention back to the General's remarks.

"Go and enjoy the peace and love of home," General Briggs said. He looked around at the soldiers and their families before continuing. "You've earned it."

The troops cheered as General Briggs stepped away. Then Colonel Spelman took the podium long enough to thank the troops and shout, "Welcome home!" He turned the podium over to the sergeant major, who told the soldiers that work call would be at 1000 tomorrow, warned them not to drink too much, and advised them not to spend all the money they'd saved on their first week back home. Finally, the sergeant major yelled, "Fall out!" Hank took a deep breath and stepped out of ranks.

Pandemonium ensued as families rushed onto the floor of the

hangar. As Hank looked around, a toddler broke free from her mother's hand and attached herself to his leg. She called out, "Da-da!" as Hank made eye contact with her.

"Sorry! Right uniform, wrong Da-da," said the little girl's mother as she scooped the toddler up and smoothed her hair.

"No problem, ma'am," Hank said with a nervous chuckle. "Military toddlers just do that when they see a camouflaged leg."

Hank looked around, his heart beating a rapid rhythm. He still did not see Sabine. Finally, through the chaos of waving hands, scuttling feet, and tearful embraces, she appeared, almost like a character from a dream, strolling toward him. Hank caught his breath and smiled when he saw that she wore the Costa Rican sun dress and the red Afghan shawl. Although the other wives and girlfriends shrieked or cried, Sabine just smiled as she strode deliberately toward him.

Sabine wrapped her arms around him gently, just as the wind shifted directions to blow directly into the hangar, lifting her long chestnut-colored hair and tossing it around them like a warm, dark curtain. Her embrace tightened, warming him from the cool October breeze. He knew the pens in his breast pocket must be hurting her, still she did not relax her silent embrace.

"Welcome home," she whispered in Hank's ear, her voice soft as crushed velvet and her breath as warm as a summer breeze. "Ich liebe dich."

"Ich liebe dich auch," he replied. "Sabine, you have no idea how good it is to be home."

"Thank God for getting you home safely," she said, her voice still soft and slow. Hank leaned his head back and looked into her eyes.

"You look beautiful. And you wore the Costa Rican sun dress."

"Do you remember the first time I wore it?"

"Of course, but what I'm thinking about right now is the first time I took it off of you."

Sabine sighed. "I remember that night." She pulled him closer and lay her head against his chest.

"A slice of heaven. That's what this day is," Hank said, as Sabine relaxed her embrace. She stepped back and examined him.

"A slice of pie is what I thought you were going to say," Sabine said, poking Hank's belly and giggling. "You've lost weight."

"Welcome home, Dad," a young man said. At first, Hank did not realize that the comment was directed at him, but when he did, he reluctantly let go of Sabine and stepped toward the sound of the voice. A tall, barrel-chested young man sporting a precisely cut blond flat-top and a Marine Corps uniform held his hand out toward Hank. Hank ignored the outstretched hand and embraced the young man.

"Michael! I'm glad you could get away from Camp Lejeune today," Hank said.

"I took a day of leave. I think the Marine Corps will continue to function in my absence."

Only then did Hank notice the young woman standing two paces behind Michael, her hands crossed in front of her. She stood almost as tall as Michael's six feet, and her long blonde hair hung almost to her waist. She stepped forward gracefully and extended her right hand.

"Dad," Michael said, "this is my fiancée, Madison."

"Welcome home, Mr. McCaskill," she said as she shook Hank's hand.

She has kind eyes, Hank thought. "I'm 'Hank' to you, young lady," he said as he hugged her awkwardly. "You're even more beautiful in person than in the photo Michael sent."

Madison blushed. "You're very kind," she said.

"So, um, show me the ring," Hank said. Madison beamed as she held her left hand out. He took her hand and whistled. "What is this, the Hope Diamond? I can't believe you bought a rock like this on a Marine Corps lieutenant's pay."

"Dad, *please*. I'm doing well financially," Michael said, smiling through tightened lips.

"Son, I am overjoyed for both of you. For all of us. Anybody else hungry?"

"I am cooking you Sauerbraten for dinner tonight," Sabine replied, "so let's not get anything too heavy."

"Right, honey," Hank said with a grin. "Nothing heavy. I'm thinking steak and eggs at Pete's. With hash browns. And can you cook Maultaschen tomorrow night? With fried green tomatoes?"

"Of course, dear," Sabine replied.

"Is Pete's some sort of local secret?" Madison asked.

"It's actually Pete's Pancake Palace," Michael answered. "But everybody just calls it 'Pete's.'"

"Pete is an old Army buddy of mine," Hank said. "Used to be a cook. Got out of the Army, bought an old Waffle House and made it his own. It's good."

Michael rolled his blue eyes. "It's good if you like your grease with an extra side of cholesterol."

Hank led Sabine, Michael, and Madison through a smudged glass door and into a sunlit diner that smelled of pancake syrup, bacon, and coffee. The clear glass on the east-facing side of the diner had been replaced with a stained-glass window that softened the late morning sunlight and cast beams of color throughout the interior. On the stained-glass window hung a sign bearing the logo, "Peace, Love, and Pancakes."

"How long has it been since you had steak and eggs, Madison?" Hank asked.

"Actually, I don't think I've ever had them," she answered, but then added, "I mean, *together*."

"Pete's steak and egg breakfast puts Waffle House to shame. I have been craving this for months. Hey, Pete!"

Just then, a broad-shouldered, pink-faced man of about sixty looked up from the griddle, wiped his hands, and walked around the counter. Although his face was beaming and his smile natural, there was a hardness to his jawline and a hint of sadness in his eyes. He hustled around the counter with the athletic grace of a much younger man, but also with a slight limp. He shook Hank's hand and hugged Sabine.

"Welcome home, amigo," Pete said. "Good God, you're skinny. Didn't they feed y'all over there?"

"Yeah, but I was on this new diet. It's called the 'Desert Heat and Dysentery Diet.' You should try it."

"I already did," Pete said with a chuckle.

"How's the knee?" Hank asked.

Pete's smile faded away. "It's never going to be a hundred percent again. Lately it hurts a little worse every day."

"I hope it gets better," Hank said.

Pete shook his head. "At my age? After what I've been through? Not likely. All I'm good for any more is an occasional fishing trip and re-reading my old Tom Clancy books." He glanced over his shoulder at the griddle. "Hey, I got to go drop an order of hash browns. We'll talk more later."

Hank studied Pete's gait as he limped away. Pete was no longer a power-lifting warrior; he was now a gimpy old cook.

And I'm about to become a tomato farmer.

While they waited for their food, Sabine sipped hot tea and laid her head on Hank's shoulder. As he stroked her hair, she closed her eyes. Michael and Madison excused themselves to go to the restrooms, and Hank and Sabine sat in silence for a moment.

"Joseph said to tell you welcome home," Sabine said. "I talked to him on the telephone last night for about twenty minutes. It was good to hear his voice, but the reception was bad."

"That's normal for Nicaragua," Hank said.

"Anyway, he emailed before and after photos of that school his church group is rebuilding. Wait until you see what they've done with it. I am very proud of him, but I wish he'd come home. Nicaragua is a violent place."

"The entire planet is a violent place. We didn't raise him to be careless. He'll be fine."

"I wish Paul were here," she said as the smile faded from her face.

"He didn't answer his cell phone last night. He told me he had a training exercise this month, so I guess that's where he is. He said he might take leave in a couple of weeks and fly down here."

"He might, huh?" Hank said. "Don't worry, honey, Paul will come around when it suits him."

"I know, but I can't wait to have all my boys home again."

"It will happen."

"I know. Miss Helen from church called to say how happy she was that you were home safe. She and the pastor want you to come to church Sunday - in uniform."

"And the pastor will say that the congregation's prayers have been answered. That will demonstrate his credibility with the man upstairs."

"You could be a little kinder to Miss Helen and the pastor. They have been praying for you for the past year, and they sent care packages to your soldiers at Christmas. Abby asks about you every Sunday. She'll be glad to see you."

"Who?"

Sabine looked disappointed. "*Abby*. Abby Mercer. She and Paul went to school together. Don't you remember that girl who used to come to the house and play music with Paul? She still sings at our church."

"I'm sorry, honey, I remember the name, but I don't remember much about her except that she sings. And you know I don't much like church. I'd rather spend Sunday morning in bed with you." He put his arm around her, and she kissed him on the cheek just as Michael sat back down.

"Don't remember who?" Michael asked.

"Do you remember a girl named Abby Mercer?" Hank asked.

Michael ran a hand over his flat-top. "She's a friend of Paul's from when we were kids. Clingy *and* annoying, all in one plump little package."

"Michael!" Sabine said, flashing him a disapproving look. "She's your brother's friend."

"Sorry, Mom."

"On a more pleasant note, you and Madison remind me of your father and me when we were your age." She kissed Hank's cheek again.

"Thanks, Mom," Michael said with a hint of sarcasm offset by a smile.

"Madison seems like a sweet young lady from a good family," Hank said.

"Her dad's a real estate broker down in Charleston. They're not hurting for money."

That's not what I meant by "a good family."

Hank and Michael stood as Madison returned to the table. She sat down carefully and looked at Hank.

"What's it like having one son in the Marines and one in the Army?" Madison asked.

"It gets competitive," Hank said, grinning. "Paul's an Army infantryman at Fort Campbell. *Air Assault* infantry. The Marines don't have that."

Michael shook his head. "Whatever, Dad. Anyway, I'm up for promotion to Captain in about seven months."

"Congratulations."

"You've got a promotion coming, too, don't you? I told Madison you're due to make lieutenant colonel next year."

"I don't think I'm ever going to make lieutenant colonel now that I have an approved retirement date."

Just then, Pete appeared, his muscular arms laden with steaming plates of steak and eggs. "Hot plates, y'all, watch out," he warned.

"Really, Dad?" Michael asked. He ducked his head around Pete's forearms to look at his father's face. "You're retiring? When?"

"You?" Pete asked. "Guys like you don't retire."

Hank watched Pete walk away and then turned to Michael. "Six weeks, give or take. But, with terminal leave, I'll take off the uniform in three weeks. It's barely enough time to do all the paperwork. Your mom is already planning my formal retirement party. I know you'll be there. I hope Paul can come. I doubt Joseph will fly up from Nicaragua, but we'll invite him."

"What brought this on?" Michael asked. Sabine shot him a tight-lipped glance and a barely perceptible shake of her head.

"Seven years, one month and eight days of war," Hank answered much too quickly and a little too harshly. "That's how long I've been deployed, getting ready to deploy, recovering from deployment, or getting another unit ready to deploy. My life has been a blur."

Sabine clasped Hank's shoulder. "It's all right. You're home."

Hank's hands trembled as he unrolled his napkin from around his silverware with great care. "I have two sons in the military and one who's a missionary," he said, staring at his knife. "And I really don't want to spend another day away from my sweet wife."

"You won't," she said, still smiling. No one else spoke. Finally, Sabine added, "I think your father just needs to rest."

"And to grow tomatoes," Hank added.

Hank waved at a neighbor as Sabine drove down the hill and turned left onto their street. As they passed a large oak tree, a two-story red brick colonial with a big front porch came into view. The sight of the red brick pulled his memories back to the time when he and Sabine had bought the house. He recalled the realtor, an overly-made-up middle-aged woman with an exaggerated southern accent, insisting they could afford something larger.

Behind the house, a privacy fence draped in wisteria stretched to the back of the property, where it disappeared beneath shadows of oak, sweetgum, and beech. In front, beds of azaleas hid the lower trunks of dogwood trees, which in turn lay clustered around a mix of yellow pines and live oaks. A row of confederate jasmine ran along each side of the walkway, beckoning Hank forward. Two large white rocking chairs beckoned from the front porch, as if awaiting his return.

"The house looks great. You've been working hard. Did you refinish the rocking chairs?"

"Yes, but it wasn't that hard. I also refinished the glider on the back porch. I had lots of time with you deployed."

Hank felt a pang of guilt. "Well, no more deployments for me. In fact, I'll probably be getting on your nerves after a while, I'm going to be around the house so much. I can't wait to see the tomato plants."

He looked to the right of the house and studied a knee-high swath of grass where a tractor path led into the forest and down to his neighbor's cornfields. Clouds, dark with the promise of rain, drifted above the treetops.

Hank thought about planting and harvesting. "Did Willie plant corn again on the other side of the woods?"

"Yes, of course. He plants corn every year."

"I didn't know if he would plant anything this year. He's getting old. Anyway, I can't wait to go for a walk in the woods. Didn't see much in the way of bottom-land hardwood forests in Iraq."

Hank walked into the foyer and set his bags down. He glanced around at the photographs that adorned the walls — his sons, his brother and sister, his parents, and Sabine's family — but the photograph of his and Sabine's wedding held his gaze. The mirror beside it showed an aging man. Hank leaned over to compare the face in the mirror to the face of the young man in the wedding photo.

He didn't look all that old - except for the eyes. His bright, hazel-green eyes were book-ended by crow's feet, the slowly etched scars of decades of work and worry. No, he didn't look old, just worn out and misplaced. He sighed, picked up one of his bags, and looked up the long staircase.

"I really, really, really don't want to go to work tomorrow," he said. Instead of climbing the stairs, he stood in the foyer, his eyes closed, soaking in the sounds and smells of home. Even the rattling of the refrigerator motor sounded like a welcoming voice.

7

Beside a dark country road about seventy miles east of Charlotte, a tall man with pale blue eyes waited in a parked Toyota Camry. Five minutes passed with no cars driving by. The man watched the rain spatter against his reflection in the windshield and, with his trigger finger, traced the track of one drop's progress down the glass.

He sang an old Lou Reed song, his voice raspy, yet his enunciation precise. Just then, his cell phone rang. He looked at the number on the caller ID and nodded.

"We're good to go," he said into the phone and hung up without waiting for a response. He powered off his phone and removed the battery just as headlights lit up his car from behind. A Dodge Caravan pulled off the road behind him, its tires squishing in the mud. The blue-eyed man drew a pistol - a stainless steel Kimber M1911 with rosewood grips - from a hip holster and slipped it into the pocket of his rain jacket. Smiling, he walked back to the minivan, peered in the window, and studied the five young men inside. The driver remained calm, but three were nervous, and one was frightened. The blue-eyed man stared at the frightened man and then motioned for the driver to lower his window.

"Are you Iqbal?" he asked the frightened man.

"Yes, sir."

The blue-eyed man studied Iqbal's face – his cat-like eyes and his slender hands. "Amal," he said to the driver, "Make sure everyone has turned off their cell phones and removed the batteries."

The driver nodded. "I saw each one of them do it, just like you said."

The blue-eyed man kept staring at Iqbal. "Follow me to the gate."

He returned to his car without waiting for a response and then drove about four miles, glancing frequently into his rearview mirror. In front of a locked gate that blocked a muddy driveway, he parked the Camry. When the van pulled in behind him, he unlocked the gate and drove up the driveway to a dilapidated farmhouse that lay hidden behind a line of trees. The minivan followed.

When the minivan stopped, the blue-eyed man spoke to Amal. "Make sure your van can't be seen from the road. The guns and the ammunition are in the trunk. I brought a couple of nine-millimeter pistols, two 12-gauge shotguns, and a couple of AKs. You can pick whatever weapons you like. Take the weapons and ammo into the house, but don't chamber any rounds."

"Understood," Amal answered.

"And look out for rats," the blue-eyed man added. He then walked down the driveway and locked the gate. He looked along the road in both directions and listened. Moments later, he walked up the driveway. The young men stood crowded around the trunk of the Camry, fawning over the pistols, rifles, and shotguns. None of them turned as he approached. The blue-eyed man drew the M1911 from the pocket of his rain jacket, held it with both hands, and fired a single round into the mud.

The men jumped and spun around.

"Lesson one," he said, "always pay attention to your surroundings.

That includes knowing what could be behind you. Get your heads in the game, starting *now*. This is not a boys' club. This is not some sort of hobby. We are training for jihad. Understand?"

The young men glanced at each other and then nodded.

Inside the farmhouse, the blue-eyed man motioned for the five men to sit on the rotting furniture strewn about the living room. As they settled in, he lit three oil lamps and set them on the end tables and the coffee table.

The blue-eyed man remained standing. "Lesson two," he said, "always remember why you're here. You're here because you felt moved to answer the call, the Dawa. You're here because you volunteered. No one tricked you or coerced you. You're here because you want to train to become mujahideen."

"Yes!" Bilal exclaimed.

"*Why* do you want this?" The blue-eyed man cast his gaze at each of the men. "Because *right now*, the United States and Britain control crusader states in Egypt, Jordan, and Lebanon. *Right now*, the United States supports the apostate regime in Saudi Arabia. *Right now*, Americans are killing Muslims in Iraq, Afghanistan, Pakistan, Yemen, and Somalia. Everywhere there is conflict between Muslims and the Kuffar, the United States is there to support the enemies of Islam. Just sixty years ago, the Zionists established their own crusader state in the heart of Palestine. Access to the al Aqsa Mosque is controlled not by waqf, but by Zionist politicians.

"You will hear some of our brothers claim we must fight the Jews. I intend no disrespect to these brothers, because they recognize that the Jews of today are just like the Jews who lived in the time of the Prophet, Peace be upon Him. But these brothers are mistaken. The way to end the Zionist regime, the way to abolish the rule of the apostates over Muslim lands, and the way to end the killing of Muslims by American technology is to attack America itself."

Iqbal looked at the faces of the men around him, his eyes wide.

"How do we do this?" the blue-eyed man continued, in excellent English. "Do we go off to fight in Iraq or Afghanistan? No. We do this another way. By the mercy of Allah, we live in the belly of the beast. We eat, sleep, and work among the ranks of the infidel. So, we will train to conduct jihad from within their own land. We will inflict a thousand cuts on America. As we do, an army of faithful brothers will rise and join us. We will attack until America falls or withdraws its support for crusader states, apostate regimes, and the enemies of Islam."

Three hours later, by the flickering light of oil lamps, they had learned the basic operations of the Glock 19 pistols, Remington 870 shotguns, and AK-47s. The highlight of the evening had been when the young men had stood in the living room and fired the Glock pistols at targets taped to the inside of a cardboard-covered window frame.

Now they chatted as they cleaned the guns. During a lull in the conversation, the blue-eyed man pulled Iqbal aside and into the kitchen. "You need to be even more careful than the others," he whispered. He reached into a cupboard, retrieved a Ziploc bag, and tossed it to Iqbal. Inside was a cell phone and charger.

"This is a burner phone. Use it to communicate with me. Don't *ever* use your personal phone, not even in an emergency. Don't visit jihadist websites using your laptop. Don't attend mosque regularly. Talk to your Christian classmates. Be polite, even when they show their true nature, which is hatred of Muslims. Act interested in Christianity but stay non-committal. Be seen having beer or wine occasionally. Get a copy of Sayyid Qutb's book *Milestones*. Buy it at a bookstore far from where you live. Pay cash. Don't just read it, *study* it."

"Yes, sir," Iqbal said. His eyes widened as the blue-eyed man studied him.

"I look forward to training you, Iqbal. You are the future of jihad."

8

Dust particles danced on a beam of golden sunlight that streamed through the window. Sabine lay wrapped around Hank, gripping him with both arms and both legs.

"Time to get up," she whispered.

"Good morning, beautiful," he said. "I would get up, but there's this one-hundred-and-twenty-pound octopus. It has me pinned to the bed. Now, this octopus is cleverly disguised as my wife, but I tell you, it's an octopus. I can't move. I can barely breathe. By the way, what time is it?"

"It's time to get up," she said. "I already told you."

"All right. But after I retire, you need to let me sleep as late as I want."

"Why?"

"Because I'm tired, Sabine. Seriously worn out."

She looked into his eyes and relaxed her hold on him. She brushed his hair with her fingers and kissed him on the cheek.

"Lie here as long as you like, then."

"Thanks. You know, it's not like I have to worry about getting kicked out of the army at this point."

"Are you sure you're ready to retire?"

"Absolutely."

"Your friend Joe Gilliland retired three years ago and did not work at all. A year after he retired, he became an alcoholic. A year after that, he shot himself."

"That's because his wife left him, not because he retired."

"She left because Joe became an alcoholic. And I think he became an alcoholic because he missed the Army." Sabine got out of bed and put on the pink silk kimono that Hank had brought her from Japan. "I know how you are, Hank. You need something to keep you occupied. Otherwise, you'll go crazy."

"I'm already crazy, honey," Hank said with a grin. "I'm crazy about *you*. What would I have to do to get you out of that kimono and back into bed?"

Sabine looked at the sunshine streaming in the window and smiled. "Just promise me you'll find something to do when you retire."

"I could go back to teaching."

Sabine shut her eyes and shook her head. "My husband, the teacher. I don't know if that's a good idea. You were gone a lot when you were teaching."

"Teaching English as a second language requires travel. Everybody knows that."

"You know, a friend of mine is an ESL teacher, but she never has to travel."

"My job was different."

"Yes. You had to travel. Find something else, Mr. McCaskill," she said as she dropped the kimono to the floor. "Something that lets you spend your nights here with me."

Hank admired his wife's figure. "Honey, you drive a tough bargain," he said. "But I'll take it."

Sixty minutes, two cups of coffee, and one long, hot shower later, Hank and Sabine were sitting in the newly refinished glider on the back porch, holding hands in the sunlight of a pleasantly cool October morning. Sabine read from her Bible for a few minutes and then closed it and leaned against Hank's side. Hank smiled as he looked across their back yard at the tomato plants and then at the majestic old oaks beyond the fence.

He studied the tomato plants. "The tomato vines are way past their prime, but next year's crop is going to be good. Some of the late-season volunteers are still green. The ones you don't fry I could make into chowchow."

Sabine sipped her green tea. "I married a hillbilly."

"Hillbilly? I prefer to think of myself as an Appalachian American, just like you're a German-American."

"Like I said, a hillbilly."

"At least I'm an educated hillbilly. I'm also a bit of a nerd."

"Hmmm," she said as she nuzzled Hank's neck. "I never would have known."

"And this nerdy old hillbilly is going to restore that old Camaro this winter. Next spring, we're going to drive it to the beach with the top down."

"It's enough just having you back home. Do you really *have* to go to work today and to that party Friday night?"

"An hour ago, you were concerned about my being home all the time. Now you're complaining that I have to leave."

Sabine smiled. "Love is strange like that, isn't it?"

"Indeed. As for the party, we don't *have* to go. However, it would be bad form for me to skip it since I'm the one who directed Lieutenant Upton to plan it."

"Can't I just keep you here as my prisoner for a while?" she asked, a twinkle in her eye.

"Well, you could, but I'd like to get all my post-deployment administrative stuff taken care of. We'll most likely be done by 1430, and then I'm all yours. Friday will be an easy day, too. Hey, did you hear that?"

"What?" Sabine asked.

"Willie's dogs. They're after something in the woods somewhere."

"Never mind those dogs," Sabine said. "You belong to me for the next hour."

9

After enduring two days of administrative briefings and enjoying a Friday evening dinner of Sabine's Maultaschen and fried green tomatoes, Hank stood in front of the full-length mirror in the master bedroom. He studied his face, focusing first on his tired eyes and then on his loose-fitting green polo shirt.

"I must've lost at least twenty pounds," he moaned.

"You'll gain it back in a month if you keep eating the way you did today," she replied from the bathroom.

He looked at the mirror again just as a popping sound from downstairs startled him. He reached down to his right thigh where he had carried his M9 Beretta.

"That was an ice cube falling into the tray," Sabine said as she stepped into the bedroom. She brushed Hank's hair back from his forehead and kissed his cheek. She stood beside him and looked at their reflections in the mirror.

Hank relaxed his right arm. "I'm sorry, honey."

"It's normal for you to be jumpy for a while."

"I just feel naked without a weapon."

He walked over to the bed, reached underneath, and punched a code into a small touchpad safe. He took out his pistol — a Heckler & Koch 45 — and held it up. His H&K was lighter but had more recoil than his army-issued Beretta, and he would need some range time to reacquaint himself with it. He cleared the pistol, slapped a magazine into the magazine well, and slipped the pistol into a concealed carry holster. He clipped the holster into place on his right hip and checked to see if it made a noticeable bulge. Then he drew the pistol and replaced it in the holster several times to get a feel for the shorter barrel and quicker draw.

Sabine watched him and shook her head. "Okay, Rambo," she said, "if you are going to drink tonight, you can't carry that. At least not legally."

"Yeah, I know." Hank unclipped the holster and put the pistol back into the gun safe with a wistful look. "I just feel naked without a weapon." He reached back into the safe and pulled out Sabine's Glock 26.

"Do you want to carry yours, honey?"

"Not really," Sabine said before looking thoughtfully at Hank. "But if it makes you feel better, I can keep it in my purse."

"Thanks."

Sabine slid the Glock into her purse and stood close to Hank. She looked into his eyes.

"I have to ask you something," she said. "What's bothering you? Something that happened over there?"

Reads me like a book. Always has. "Yeah. There was this bad guy named Abu Ghazali. His idea of a good time was planting IEDs, and launching rockets at Americans, and..." Hank's voice trailed off.

Sabine rubbed his shoulder. "And?"

Hank felt like he was being choked. He closed his eyes and shook his head.

"It's fine if you don't want to talk about it," Sabine said.

"The things that man did were ... beyond the pale." Hank shivered and clenched his fists.

Sabine nudged him toward the bed. "It's also fine if you *do* want to sit down and talk about it."

"I don't want to sit down, but yeah, I'll talk about it. Abu Ghazali had his men kidnap two girls. They were sisters. One was fourteen, and the other was sixteen. He ... he had his men rape both girls. Then Abu Ghazali persuaded the girls that getting raped was their fault. Then he told them that the only way Allah would forgive them was for them to martyr themselves. This would also save their family's honor. His men gave the girls drugs, strapped suicide vests on them, and sent them walking into two police stations in Shi'a neighborhoods. An Iraqi policeman spotted the older sister as she approached and – God, that man was brave – he stopped her outside the station and talked to her until his wife came. His wife persuaded the girl to take off the vest and turn herself in."

Hank opened his eyes and looked at the ceiling. "The younger sister ... the younger sister wasn't so lucky. Anyway, Abu Ghazali is still at large. I prayed that God would deliver him into my hand, but that didn't happen. And on our last day there, I thought we had him." Hank's eyes turned hot and wet as he squinted. "But he slipped through our fingers. Again."

"It doesn't make you less of a man if you cry about it."

"I'm not much of a crier. I'm just angry and disappointed."

"So that's it. You're thinking about a bad guy. The one that got away. I won't ask you to forget about him because I know you can't do that. And I won't tell you to get over it because it's not that simple. But I will tell you that you need to find a constructive way to deal with your anger and disappointment."

Hank smiled. "My mental health plan includes one hot wife, one tomato patch, and lots of free time."

Sabine drove her Escape while Hank watched their house shrink in the rearview mirror.

"Thanks for driving, honey."

"I don't mind being the designated driver," she said. "I just don't want you to be the designated drunk." Her face and her voice conveyed a frankness that Hank understood immediately.

"Look, I was deployed for a year. I'm going to have a couple of drinks with my guys, and that's all. Don't worry, I won't do anything stupid."

"I remember how much you used to drink when we first met. It was too much. Even by German standards, you drank too much."

"And your people have high standards when it comes to drinking."

She shot him a cold glance.

"Sorry," Hank said. "You made me see that I needed to change, and I changed. That's just one more reason I love you."

Sabine winked and smiled. "Nice recovery."

Hank started to say something more, but his cell phone rang. He answered and immediately held the phone away from his ear as music and laughter crackled from the speaker.

Chapman's voice boomed from the phone. "Hey, sir, I've got you on speakerphone," he said above the din of music that sounded vaguely like Nickelback. "The lieutenant and I were wondering, could you pick up a six-pack of Blue Moon on the way over here? The lieutenant has this hot little girlfriend who won't drink anything else."

"Only if you change the music before we get there."

"All right. I'll let Litton pick the playlist."

"I don't know—"

"By the way, sir," Chapman interrupted, "your soldiers have been talking smack about you. Decker says he's smarter than you, Davis says he could beat you like a rented mule if you ever gloved up against him, and Litton said he could kill you five-to-one in Halo. But I said, hey, the major's pretty good. For a man his age, anyway." At that, a chorus of raucous laughter erupted from Hank's phone, prompting Hank to hang up.

Sabine drove past a convenience store where Hank occasionally stopped to buy beer on his way home. This convenience store also brewed excellent coffee, which Hank appreciated. Hank saw one car parked in front of the store.

"Honey, let's stop here and get some beer."

After passing the convenience store, Sabine turned into the parking lot of a grocery store that stood behind it.

"You walk over and get some beer. I'll get some club soda and a vegetable tray. You know they never have anything healthy at these things. I'll pick you up when I'm done."

"Promise you won't leave me there?"

"Not this time. But if you get drunk tonight, I may leave you there on my way home," she said with mock seriousness.

"I love you," he said as he leaned over to kiss her. "If I get drunk tonight, it will be from the magical elixir of your sweet, sweet love."

Sabine laughed and shook her head as she parked the Escape.

Hank trotted across the parking lot and into the convenience store. A thin man in his early thirties stood propped against the counter, flipping through a *Sports Illustrated*.

"What's going on, Tommy?" Hank asked.

"Hey, Hank. I haven't seen you in, what, nine months or so?"

"Almost a year. I just got back from Iraq yesterday morning."

"Glad you made it back safe," Tommy said before standing upright to shake Hank's hand.

"I'm surprised to see you're still here. If this company had any sense, they would have promoted you to district manager by now. What's new around here?"

"About an hour ago our external security camera quit working. They're sending someone out to fix it tomorrow. Otherwise, it's a slow night."

"Do y'all still stock Blue Moon?"

"Yeah. If there's not any on display, you can walk back in the cooler and check."

Hank didn't see any on display, so he entered the walk-in cooler, shivered, and began singing the words to "Blue Moon." Three cases of Blue Moon sat on the floor beside a set of hand trucks. Hank picked up a case and turned to exit. He continued singing, "... suddenly appeared before me—"

"Don't nobody move," someone yelled. Hank stopped singing. He turned to see two men walking into the store. Both wore ski masks. Both held handguns in their right hands, and one held a can of spray paint in his left. Hank shivered and put down the case of Blue Moon so he could peer out from between the racks of beer. Keeping his gaze on the robbers, Hank reached for the Beretta that no longer hung on his thigh. He then reached back to his right hip and remembered that his H&K 45 was in the safe under the bed. He clenched his hands into fists and stepped toward the display racks.

Be the best witness you can be, Hank told himself. He looked through his own ghostly reflection in the cooler door and focused on the robbers. Both wore ski masks and latex gloves, but he could see enough skin around their eyes to tell that one was tall and white, the other short and black. The tall white man stood to the side of the counter with an M1911 pointed at Tommy's head, while the short black man checked each aisle over the sights of a nine-millimeter Glock.

Since he was unarmed, Hank's tactical sense told him to crouch and hide. He crept toward a dark section of the cooler, but then leaned forward and watched as the tall white man held the can of spray paint toward Tommy.

"Spray the lens of your security camera," he said. His voice was calm but commanding, youthful but raspy - a distinctive voice that Hank would remember. Tommy took the can and sprayed the camera, his hand trembling. The tall man then moved around in front of the register. Tommy stood with his hands overhead, still clutching the can of spray paint.

The tall man leaned across the counter toward Tommy. "Put the can down."

"Yes sir," Tommy said.

"You sure we're all clear?" the tall man asked his accomplice.

"All clear," the accomplice said and then moved closer to the door.

"Play nice, *Tommy*," the tall man said.

Tommy shrank back, but said nothing.

The tall man continued. "I know you have an alarm button under the counter. If you touch it, you die. Empty the contents of the register into a bag but keep your hands where I can see them at all times."

Tommy nodded and lowered his trembling hands toward the register but never took his eyes off the man's pistol.

"Just follow instructions," the tall man said. "We'll be out of here in a minute. You can go home alive tonight."

Hank studied the two men, starting with the accomplice, working from the head downward, just like he had been trained in counterintelligence school. *Subject one, appearance: Black male, five-seven, heavy build, weight about 220. Armed with automatic pistol, looks like a nine-millimeter Glock. Activity: watching the aisles and the door. Role: accomplice. Disposition: angry, impulsive.*

Subject two, appearance: White male, six foot two, thin build, weight about 190. Also armed with an automatic, looks like a M1911, stainless steel. Activity: Robbing the cashier. Role: leader. Disposition: calm, methodical. But that voice is unique, almost like a fingerprint.

Tommy's hands shook so badly that he dropped a handful of bills as he tried to stuff the cash into a plastic bag.

"Shoot that punk," the accomplice snapped. "He's trying to play us!"

"Easy," the tall man said.

"Let me shoot him, then!" the accomplice said. He took a step toward the register and pointed his Glock at Tommy.

"No. We're here for the cash," the tall man said. "Cover our six and be quiet."

Hank dropped to a crouch and crept back to the cooler door. He took the cell phone from his pocket, set it to camera mode, and raised it slowly.

Tommy fumbled with the register, his hands shaking even more violently than before. "Oh, Jesus," he muttered as he dropped a handful of coins on the floor.

Hank shifted so that the height markings beside the door were in the same picture frame as the robbers, who were both pointing guns at Tommy.

Smile, boys, you're on camera.

"Never mind the small change," the tall man said. "Give me your wallet instead, or I may let my partner shoot you."

"Just say the word," the accomplice said, turning his gaze from the door to Tommy.

"That's all I got," Tommy stammered as he laid his wallet on the counter.

"Take off that watch and ring or I'm gonna waste you!" the accomplice yelled.

Tommy cringed and closed his eyes. "Oh, Jesus," he whimpered.

"Settle down," the tall man said. "Shut up and watch the door."

Hank snapped the photo. As he did, a flash of light illuminated the cooler and Hank saw his reflection in the glass. For an instant, he was perplexed, but then he realized what had gone wrong. He had forgotten to disable the flash.

10

Hank rolled to his right just before the cooler door exploded and bullets slammed into the wall behind him. Glass cubes sprayed into the cooler as he scrambled away on his elbows and knees. Above him, beer cans burst and wine bottles shattered, showering Hank with liquid, and littering the floor with glass shards. The gunfire rattled around him like a jackhammer, but Hank focused on counting the shots. At least eleven. He scrambled to the back corner of the cooler and picked up an intact wine bottle. Blood trickled from his hands and knees, but he felt no pain as he hefted the bottle overhead and tested its weight.

"Let's go," the tall man yelled.

Hank gritted his teeth as footsteps approached the cooler door. A gloved hand slipped inside. The accomplice pushed it open a few inches, but the door jammed on the glass that littered the floor. A black pistol barrel darted into the open door and pointed in Hank's direction. Hank turned his right side toward the door and flattened himself against the racks. The pistol slipped back out of the cooler and the man shoved the door with his shoulder. The door crunched open another inch. Hank gripped the wine bottle as if it were the hilt of a sword. He crouched and waited.

"I said let's go," the tall man yelled.

The accomplice didn't respond; he just slammed his shoulder into the cooler door. The door crunched open by a fraction of an inch. Again and again, he slammed his shoulder into the door, and, inch by inch, it crunched open. The gloved hand and pistol snaked into the cooler, followed by a shoulder and then a masked head. With one final heave, the man shoved the door all the way open and stepped into the cooler. Instead of raising his pistol, the man fidgeted with the magazine release catch. Hank heard the scrape of steel on steel he had been waiting for. The man was changing magazines.

Hank launched himself forward and raised the wine bottle overhead. The accomplice slammed a fresh magazine home and raised his pistol just as Hank grabbed the pistol with his left hand and swung the bottle with his right. The man twisted and jabbed his left forearm into Hank's right. Still, the bottle struck the man's head with a thud, twisted out of Hank's grasp, fell to the floor, and shattered. The man crumpled and dropped his pistol into a puddle of wine and glass. Hank scooped up the wet pistol and darted through the cooler door. When he scanned across the sights in the direction of the register, he caught a glimpse of icy blue eyes staring at him through the holes of a ski mask. A silver pistol jerked in his direction.

Hank ducked. A gunshot thundered in front of him, and a round struck behind him, sending bags of potato chips flying. Hank tiptoed to his left and leaned around a rack of beef jerky. He tried to get a sight picture on the tall man, but the man ducked behind an adjacent aisle. A flash of movement caught Hank's eye. Tommy was crouched behind the counter, jabbing an index finger toward the door.

Hank stepped around the aisle to see the tall man's back as he ran out of the store. Hank snapped the pistol upward and placed the front sight post on the tall man's back. He tightened his grip but didn't squeeze the trigger. The man pivoted hard to the right before being swallowed by the night.

A second later, two popping sounds came from the front of the store. Bullets whizzed by, striking among the pain relievers and cold medications. Hank dropped to the floor as pill bottles tumbled off shelves and sticky purple liquids dribbled to the floor. Another round slammed into the cash register with a ringing sound that echoed like a mockery of a church bell. Another bullet buzzed past, but Hank could not tell where it struck. Hank crawled toward the door, eyes scanning for the shooter, but didn't see him. That meant that he was reloading.

Hank sprang forward and knocked the door open with his left hand. Pivoting hard to his left, he dropped to one knee beside a garbage can. He scanned the parking lot over the sights of the Glock but saw nothing. Then he heard the rapid slap-slap of boots striking the pavement.

Part of Hank's mind told him to stay put, but another part told him to follow the man and kill him. He scanned to his front and right. The night was calm, surreal. Only the sounds of crickets singing disturbed the silence. Hank rose, tiptoed to his right and stepped two paces back from the corner of the store. He darted forward, peering around the corner over the pistol's sights. A figure crouched there in the shadows, looking down. Hank lined up the sights and squeezed the trigger.

The tall man jerked to the left as Hank's bullet punched a hole in a metal drum. Instead of taking a second shot, Hank ducked back around the corner of the store. A car approached from behind, but Hank forced himself to stay focused on the corner. Two bullets zipped past just in front of him, and Hank hustled back to the garbage can, dropped to one knee, and waited with the pistol braced against the garbage can's top. From here he had a twenty-foot line of sight to the corner, a partial view of the parking lot, and a view of one section of road.

Seconds crawled by and Hank's hands began to shake. The only sound seemed to be his own breathing. Just as Hank was about to stand, a figure dashed toward the road, the silver pistol in his hand. Hank tried to take aim, but the man zig-zagged through the shadows and reached the road just as car headlights illuminated the storefront behind Hank.

Moves like a cat, Hank thought as he raised his left hand to shield his eyes from the glare.

Although hitting a moving target at night with an unfamiliar hand-gun was nearly impossible, Hank squeezed off a shot in the direction the tall man had fled. There was only a wooded lot there, so he didn't worry about collateral damage. Then Hank heard a car door open and an engine starting. He saw only shadows until a series of flashes illuminated the tall man firing a rifle. The unmistakable, staccato sound of 5.56-millimter rounds followed. Bullets struck the parking lot, slammed into the gas pump, and shattered the storefront window. Concrete fragments sprayed around Hank as he dove to the pavement. He rolled up against the raised concrete beside a gas pump and squeezed off two more shots. The car careened out of the woods and onto the road without headlights. Hank rose to a crouch and raised the pistol but held his fire because another car was pulling out of a nearby parking lot.

Hank stood and cursed as the silence surged back over the store, but then the sound of a car idling behind him broke his train of thought. He turned around to find Sabine's Escape parked in front of the store, the radio playing softly. The driver's side door was ajar, and the window was shattered, pierced by a single bullet hole. Hank's heart stopped.

"Dear God, no," Hank muttered as he sprinted to the SUV. He stumbled to a halt at the car door and dropped the pistol. He yanked the door open and found Sabine slumped over the steering wheel. "Sabine!" he yelled, but she did not respond.

At first glance, she looked like she was sleeping, except for a small bloodstain on the left side of her blouse. Hank tore open Sabine's blouse and examined her side. She groaned but did not move. There was surprisingly little blood on her side, and only a small entry wound. He slipped his right hand around her back to check for an exit wound.

There, his fingers encountered a warm, soft mass of blood and shredded tissue. He checked her breathing and found her respiration slow, but discernible. Next, he checked her carotid pulse and detected a faint, irregular flutter. Just then, the entry wound on her side made a whooshing sound and bubbled a pink froth.

"Listen, honey, you've been shot through the lung. I'm going to pull you toward me so you're on your left side with the injured lung down. If you can hear me, squeeze my hand."

Hank felt an almost imperceptible squeeze on his hand. There was still hope. As he laid her on her side, he prayed aloud, "God, don't take her yet, not before me."

Hank realized Tommy was standing behind him. "Call 911! Get an ambulance!" he yelled. He dashed to the rear of the Escape and pulled out a nylon bag. He dug inside and tossed aside a flashlight and a set of jumper cables before finding the first aid kit. With the kit in hand, he went back to Sabine's side, where he plucked out an Israeli pressure dressing, gauze, and tape. He ripped open the sterile package and applied the pressure dressing to the exit wound on Sabine's back.

"You're going to be okay, honey," Hank said, thinking that she might be able to hear him. "I'm going to put tape over the entry wound to keep air from getting into your thorax."

He squeezed her hand again when he was done. *Probably too hard.* He relaxed his grip and prayed. He was not sure how much time had passed when he realized that Tommy was standing behind him again and that Jimmy Buffet's *"Come Monday"* was playing on the radio.

"I called an ambulance," Tommy said.

"Thank you," Hank mumbled.

"That guy you clubbed is still in the store. I got some duct tape and taped his hands behind his back. Are you okay? Did you get shot? Your knees and hands are bleeding."

Hank did not acknowledge Tommy's questions. Instead, he knelt beside Sabine, holding her hand and choking back the volcanic rage rising in his chest. *No, God, not before me!*

The song on the radio seemed to mock him. He kicked at the pistol that lay on the asphalt and cursed as he glanced at his watch. Finally, his eyes fell upon Sabine's purse, which lay open on the console. Her Glock lay on the passenger floorboard, beside the jumbled contents of a vegetable tray. She had been coming to help him.

Seven minutes later, two police cars squealed to a stop in the parking lot, followed a minute later by an ambulance. Hank knelt, holding Sabine's hand, and weeping. When he looked up, a police officer with Sergeant stripes on his sleeve was talking to Tommy. Tommy said something that caused the Sergeant to shout and point. One officer walked around the store with his weapon drawn. Then the Sergeant pointed in the direction the tall man had fled. The second pair of police officers scrambled into their car and drove away in pursuit. Finally, the Sergeant pointed the paramedics toward Hank.

As the paramedics unfolded a stretcher, Hank fought the urge to tell them to hurry. He knew that a systematic approach was the most likely to save Sabine's life. Still, it felt like an eternity until the stretcher clattered to a halt beside him. He let go of Sabine's hand, stood, and stepped back.

"My wife has been shot," Hank said, surprising himself at how calm he sounded. "One bullet, lower left lung. There's a large exit wound on her back."

The first paramedic checked Sabine's respiration and pulse while the second checked the pressure dressing. Although they talked to each other, neither spoke to Hank. Hank said a quick prayer, knowing that if she arrived at an emergency room within an hour, she had a fighting chance. Hank clasped her hand again and walked alongside the stretcher as the paramedics wheeled her to the ambulance. He tried to speak some words of comfort and assurance, but words failed him. She still had a pulse when he kissed her hand and let go.

"*Ich liebe dich,*" Hank whispered despite the squeezing sensation in his chest.

As the paramedics loaded Sabine in the ambulance, more police officers arrived. The Sergeant leaned into a police car's open window, alternately talking on the radio and directing the officers around him. Two officers began combing through the store. They cuffed the man that Hank had clubbed, searched his pockets, and removed the tape. Another officer began stretching yellow tape around the parking lot.

Hank looked away from the ambulance as a blue Crown Victoria with a flashing blue light on the dash came squealing to a halt. The Crown Vic passed dangerously close to the police officer who was cordoning the parking lot, earning its driver an angry scowl. Two men stepped out and approached Hank, both dressed in slacks and collared shirts with clip-on ties. One was plump, pale, and sweaty; the other lean, muscular, and tan.

"I'm Detective Ballinger," the plump man said, "and this is Detective Agosto." The men flashed badges in front of Hank. He nodded but didn't look at the badges.

"You are ...?" Detective Agosto asked.

"Major William Henry McCaskill, United States Army. Almost retired. I go by 'Hank.'"

"Major McCaskill, did you witness what happened here?" Agosto asked.

"Yes, but can it wait? I'd like to go to the hospital with my wife."

"Tell you what," Ballinger said, pointing toward the Crown Vic with his chin, "I'll drive you to the hospital. We can talk on the way. Maybe you saw something that can help us catch this guy."

Hank started to say that he'd drive himself, but the parking lot had already been cordoned off. Sabine's Escape was inside a perimeter of yellow tape. He looked up when the ambulance turned on its siren and sped away. As he stumbled toward Detective Ballinger's car, a cold realization washed over him. *She may already be dead.*

11

Detective Ballinger didn't follow the ambulance. He drove fast, but not recklessly, and did not turn on the flashing light. He asked Hank a few innocuous questions mixed in with questions about what Hank was doing in the convenience store, and whether he had been drinking, then his demeanor changed.

"Did you get a look at the guy that got away, or getaway car, or anything like that?"

"He wore a ski mask, and he had pale blue eyes. He had a raspy voice. I didn't see a getaway car."

Ballinger made a radio call to Agosto, telling him they did not have a good description of the shooter or of a getaway car. He slumped his shoulders forward in apparent resignation. "Armed robbers are some of the dumbest, most violent criminals you can encounter. I'm sorry about your wife."

Hank's attention was split between his wife and the glass fragments that remained in his hands and knees, but he managed to say, "Thank you."

"You know, Agosto and I were working late on an unrelated case when the call came in, so we came out as fast as we could. I wish we had gotten there sooner."

Hank nodded and shivered as he picked the last glass fragment out of the heel of his right hand. There was little blood. Hank's adrenaline surge began to wear off and a chill settled onto his skin.

"You smell like you took a shower in cheap wine and beer," Ballinger said with a tentative grin.

"More of baptism, actually," Hank said without looking at Ballinger. He gazed out the window at the lights of the houses they passed and wondered if the blue-eyed man were hiding in one of them.

At the hospital, Ballinger marched into the ER, staying one full step ahead of Hank. Ballinger flashed his badge at the receptionist and pushed through a double door toward the sound of urgent voices. He flashed his badge again, and a security guard waved them forward.

"The gunshot patient is in trauma room three," the guard said. He turned to walk back to the ER door and added, "but I need y'all to go back to the ER waiting room after you check on the vic."

Hank collapsed onto a cold plastic chair in the deserted waiting room, the fatigue finally catching up to him. The cuts on his hands and knees began to hurt. Ballinger sat down beside Hank and looked at him with a mix of sympathy and suspicion.

"Major, I know this is a difficult time for you, but it's best if we get the facts while they're still fresh in your mind. I'd like to ask you some questions — informally — if you're up to it."

"Yeah. I'm up to it. Call me Hank."

Detective Ballinger sat close to him and pulled a small Moleskine notebook from his coat pocket.

"State your full name."

"William Henry McCaskill. Retired Army Major. I go by 'Hank.'"

"All right, um, Hank. Can you describe the man who fled the scene?"

"Yes," Hank said, surprised that Ballinger had gone straight to the suspect description.

"Go ahead."

"Adult white male. He was tall, about six-two, maybe six-three.

Thin build. Approximate weight 190 to 210. I couldn't see his hair color because of the mask."

"Slow down a second while I write this all down. Let's see, white male, six-two, pale blue eyes."

"He was wearing a red plaid shirt, like something you might wear to a Country and Western bar. It had that cut to the shoulders and those, um, fake pearl snaps instead of buttons."

"Western shirt. Got it."

"His shirt was untucked, so I couldn't see his belt or what else he was carrying. He wore faded blue jeans and old leather work boots, well broken-in."

"Slow down again, Major."

Hank waited for Ballinger to stop writing. "He wore a diver's watch on his left wrist, no wedding ring. He was armed with an automatic. It looked like a stainless steel M1911. Fired it right-handed."

"That's a solid description, Major," Ballinger said, tapping his notebook with his pen for emphasis. "Half the time when I interview a witness I have to ask, 'Was he taller than you or shorter than you?' Even then, a lot of 'em don't know."

"I worked as a counterintelligence agent for the Army for a couple of years. I wasn't the best agent who ever carried a badge, but I didn't do too badly."

"Counterintelligence, huh?" Ballinger said, raising an eyebrow. "All right then, you know something about how this is going to work. We'll see what ballistics brings back on the bullet, but it's always good if a witness can place the gun in the suspect's hand. You know much about guns?"

"Yes, and I have a concealed carry permit, but I'm not carrying tonight."

"Why not?" Ballinger asked.

"So I could drink," Hank said, wincing as he spoke.

"So, how many drinks did you have before you, um, *intervened* in this robbery?"

"None."

"Not even one?" Ballinger said, his gaze boring into Hank's eyes. "You willing to blow a breathalyzer to verify that?"

"Yes. We were on our way to a party and I had Sabine stop so I could buy some beer."

Ballinger nodded. "Okay. I believe you. We'll skip the breathalyzer. Is there anything else you'd like to add about the man who shot your wife?"

"His voice was distinctive. It was youthful, but raspy, like he had a sore throat."

"Go on," Ballinger said, his pen poised just above the page.

"I'd recognize that voice anywhere."

"Okay. Aside from his voice, is there anything further you'd like to add?"

"Yeah. He was cool under pressure."

"Cool under pressure, huh?" Ballinger said with a nod and an expression that encouraged Hank to keep talking.

"Yeah. I hate to say it, but he sounded like he might have been military. He talked like a soldier. He said, 'keep your hands where I can see them at all times.' Later, his accomplice yelled, 'All clear' when he determined the store was empty. And the blue-eyed man said to watch their six. I could tell he was in charge. He had the other man check the aisles to make sure no one was in the store while he kept his gun pointed at the cashier and gave the orders. He crouched and used a modified Weaver grip when he fired his pistol. He even had an AR-15 stashed in his getaway car."

"Military, huh? We both know your kind ain't all saints and school-boys, Major."

"No, but it hurts to think it's one of my own — a soldier — who did this."

"I feel you. That's the same way it hurts me when a cop goes bad. Any other observations, Major?"

"I'm thinking."

"Now, you said that the blue-eyed man – subject two – had subject one check the store to make sure no one was in it. How is that you were in the store and subject one didn't see you?"

"I was inside the walk-in cooler."

"*Inside* the cooler?"

"Yeah. They didn't have any Blue Moon on display, so I went into the cooler. The cashier knows me, and I've done it before. From inside the cooler, I could see out, but the robbers couldn't see in. Now that you mention it, the bad guy who cleared the store — subject one, the short man — wasn't very careful. He gave the cooler a cursory glance and called 'all clear.' He probably wasn't military."

"And then you attacked subject one with a wine bottle?"

"That was all I had. If I'd had my gun, I would have shot them both."

Detective Ballinger shifted uncomfortably in his seat. "All right, Major. Listen, just in case the District Attorney wants to charge you with something, no more comments about yourself or your motives. Let's just talk about the robber that got away so I can get this bad boy rolled up."

"Charge *me* with something?" Hank said with a trace of indignation. "Listen, I've been stopping by that store for years. I know the cashiers and I always make small talk with them. I thought those two were going to shoot Tommy."

"I understand that, and, unofficially, I'll do what I can to protect you. But let's stick to information about the one that got away."

"All right."

Ballinger wrinkled his brow and started to ask another question, but at just that moment, a nurse stuck her head around the corner. "Mr. Mack?"

"*McCaskill*," Hank answered with a little more irritation in his voice than he intended.

"I'm sorry," the nurse said before squinting at her clipboard. "Mr. McCaskill, Doctor Chan would like to talk to you now."

Hank stood up without looking at Detective Ballinger and followed the nurse to the door of trauma room three. There, a grim-faced, middle-aged Asian woman, still in her cap and scrubs, stood beside the closed door, her mask dangling in front of her like a necklace. She straightened her scrub cap as if it were a crown and looked into Hank's eyes. Hank recognized her as the woman who had scurried past them earlier and told them to leave.

"I'm Dr. Chan. You're Mr. McAllister, Sabrina's husband?"

"*McCaskill*," Hank said, again with more irritation in his voice than he intended. "And my wife's name is 'Sabine,' not 'Sabrina.' She's German."

Dr. Chan nodded. "All right, Mr. *McCaskill*. Your wife, *Sabine*, has a punctured left lung from a gunshot wound. The bullet penetrated below the left breast, passed just underneath her heart, and exited her back. She's lost a lot of blood, and I can't be sure that her heart muscle hasn't been damaged. I'm also concerned about fluid accumulation. She is unconscious, but she's alive."

"Thank God," Hank said. He exhaled deeply. "And thank *you*, Dr. Chan."

Doctor Chan raised her palm. "Let me finish. Sabine will need follow-up surgery when she stabilizes. That is, *if* she stabilizes. We can't operate right now. The left lung has collapsed, and the right is already having a problem with fluid. We will do everything we can, but you need to prepare yourself for the likelihood that she will not make it."

Her words struck Hank like a hammer blow to his chest. "What?"

"I've treated injuries like this before. Sometimes patients recover and sometimes there are complications. Her condition will be touch and go for at least the next couple of days. The first step is to get her stabilized. She has internal bleeding, which we have to stop. Then we have to get her breathing on her own. Then we can go in and look at the damage to her heart."

"But, but you said the bullet missed her heart," Hank said, his voice trembling.

"Yes, she's very fortunate. Had the bullet passed just a little closer to the heart, she would have died within a few seconds. However, the vascular pressure impulse — the cavitation — of the bullet passing through her body may have torn the aorta or injured the cardiac muscle. It could be that the swelling is holding her heart together right now. She also has some air in her thoracic cavity but not much considering the injury. I understand you administered first aid. Is that right?"

"Yes."

"You most likely saved her life, Mr. McCaskill. We'll know more tomorrow about how to proceed. If she makes it through the night—"

"*If*? Can I see her?"

"Yes, I think you should. If her heart muscle is torn — or even worse, her aorta — she could expire with little notice as the swelling subsides. We're going to move her to intensive care in a little while. As long as you don't get in the way, the ICU nurses will let you see her. But please don't stay more than a few minutes. They have other patients to consider."

Forty minutes later, Hank walked to his wife's hospital bed in the ICU. Sabine was almost unrecognizable. Her long chestnut hair was bundled under a green surgical cap, her face was obscured by a respirator, and her body lay underneath a jungle of cables and tubes. Around her stood an array of beeping, whirring machines whose purposes Hank could only guess at. He reached carefully through the plastic jungle that separated him from his wife and took her hand.

"Sabine, honey, I don't know if you can hear me, but I want you to know that I love you. Ich liebe dich. Always and no matter what." He kissed the back of her hand and then knelt to pray. Although the charge nurse was watching him, he prayed aloud. Then he stood. As he looked at her, an icy cold malice supplanted the hot rage in his chest.

In his mind, Hank played back the scene of the blue-eyed man running out of the convenience store. Hank visualized his front sight post silhouetted against the man's back as if that instant had been the pivotal moment of a great battle. But in his mental replay, Hank fired the pistol until the magazine was empty and the man lay crumpled and bleeding in the parking lot.

12

Fayetteville, North Carolina
October 18, 2008

Hank jerked awake in the cold plastic chair. He looked around at the artificial flowers on the vanity and then at the clock on the wall. It was 5:55 AM, and he was in the ICU waiting room. A nurse was telling him something. Although he could not process the words, he understood from her tone and her body language that Sabine had survived the night.

Much of the previous night had deteriorated into a blur of hospital corridors, bedside visits, and awkward telephone calls. Hank had contacted Michael at Camp Lejeune, and Paul at Fort Campbell. With some difficulty, he placed a call to Joseph in Nicaragua. He called Sabine's mother in Germany, and Brian Etheridge, the brigade executive officer he had served with in Iraq. Brian said he would help Hank with his remaining administrative requirements for retirement. He also told Hank that he would help him any time, in any way, and that all Hank had to do was ask. Hank filed that offer away.

Next, Hank called the Pastor, who offered to pray with Hank on the phone, but Hank declined. Finally, he called Miss Helen, who said she'd help with the housework and cooking while Sabine was in the hospital. To Hank's surprise, Miss Helen said that Sabine had given her a door key. In all his conversations, he maintained the charade of being calm and organized, but his trembling hands and aching stomach told a different story. He craved a cold beer, or better yet a glass of whiskey, but he refrained from drinking. Hank still had to call Sabine's supervisor at the surgery center.

Michael arrived at the hospital mid-morning. While Hank and Michael talked, Paul crept into the waiting room dressed in hiking boots and tactical pants, with a small backpack over his US Army sweatshirt. He looked like a shorter, younger, dark-haired version of Hank.

"Paul! It's good to see you, son," Hank said as he hugged his son and fought back tears.

"I've missed you, Dad," Paul said. He then hugged Michael. "I missed you too, bro, even though you're a Marine."

Michael smiled. "I missed you too, bro, but you need a haircut."

Paul tossed his backpack into a chair and turned back to Hank. "How is she?"

"Right now, only God knows, and he ain't had much to say."

Hank related the story of how Sabine had been shot. Michael grew angry and ran his hand over his flat-top while gritting his teeth. Paul, on the other hand, nodded and listened, his fists clenched and his eyes narrow. Paul's face lay impassive under his short, swept-back chestnut hair, but his heavy brow and quick green eyes gave him a fierce, wolfish appearance. Those eyes seemed to glow as Hank finished the story.

"Dad, you look exhausted," Paul said when Hank was done. "Why don't you take a break? Michael and I can stay with Mom a while, and Joseph won't be here until tomorrow evening."

"Where am I supposed to go?" Hank asked. "I can't go home."

"There's a hotel across the street," Michael said. "The ICU nurse told me that a lot of people visiting relatives in the hospital stay there."

"You're right," Hank sighed. "A shower and some sleep would do me good. Call me immediately if there's any change in your mom's condition."

Hank left the ICU and walked toward the ER, his mind replaying the moment when he had taken aim at the blue-eyed man's back. *I should have shot him.* He walked across the street to the hotel and booked a suite with a small living room and a kitchenette. There, he stumbled around, looking for his room. At last, he found himself in a sad little room that sported 1980s-style faux-leather furniture and mauve-colored vertical blinds. He sat on a scratchy acrylic bedspread, kicked his shoes off, and exhaled. He stifled a sob and studied the geometric patterns in the garish lavender wallpaper as if they were some sort of puzzle. With his hands over his eyes, he flopped onto the bed, still dressed.

He moved his hands and examined the ceiling for a moment, scowling at a faint water stain. He grabbed the pillow, forced into a suitable shape, then punched it. When his cell phone rang, he fumbled about, trying to remember where he had put it.

"Hello?"

"Major, this is Detective Ballinger. I just wanted to let you know that the young man you clubbed last night has a bad headache and some eyebrow stitches, but he doesn't appear to have any serious injuries."

"Good," Hank said. "He can be interrogated. What has he told you?"

"I'll get to that in a minute. Can you come down to the station Monday morning, fill out a written statement, sign some papers?"

"What's his name?"

Ballinger hesitated. "Funny thing is, he wouldn't tell us his name, but we identified him by his fingerprints. He resisted, but a colleague of mine named Taggert played college football, and Taggert's about as big as a house. He held the perp down and we fingerprinted him despite his, um, *objections*. Perp's name is Jamal Wilson, from up the road in Durham. Rap sheet has him for small-time theft and burglary, misdemeanor drug charges. Served a few months for aggravated assault a couple of years ago. He's in custody and he ain't going anywhere. He's been charged with robbery with a dangerous weapon and conspiracy to commit armed robbery with a dangerous weapon. Now, get some sleep and I'll see you Monday. Nine o'clock all right with you?"

"What did he tell you about his partner?"

Ballinger hesitated again, but then said, "Nada."

"Nothing at all?"

"Nope."

"Do you think he's afraid of his partner?"

Ballinger didn't reply.

"Hello?" Hank asked.

"I think it's, um, *unproductive* for us to speculate at this point. Now, can you come down here Monday morning?"

"Yeah, Monday's fine," Hank said before hanging up. He lay back on the bed, this time studying the swirling patterns in the faux glass of the light fixture instead of the geometric patterns on the wallpaper.

Hank's pulse slowed, and he had nearly fallen asleep when images of shooting the blue-eyed man began playing in front of his eyes. His mind would not obey his attempts to squelch those images or silence the blue-eyed man's voice. At last, he rose, put his shoes on, and walked across the street to the hospital. He felt and tasted the deliciously cool October air but took no joy in either sensation.

Michael had left, and Paul sat low in a waiting room chair, his eyes shut. Hank tiptoed past him and into the ICU. He held Sabine's hand, stared at the tangle of plastic tubes that seemed to hold her in place, and then knelt to pray. He stood and nodded at the charge nurse before trudging out.

Paul was sitting upright when Hank stepped back into the ICU waiting room. He said nothing, but his wolfish green eyes met Hank's with an unspoken question. Hank smiled, but then his thoughts were interrupted by the deep, resonant sound of an acoustic guitar. Despite his grief and rage, or perhaps because of it, Hank was especially sensitive to the unexpected music. The tune was a slow, soothing finger-picked guitar melody, and although it sounded familiar, he could not quite place it. As soon as the woman began to sing, however, Hank recognized the tune as *"The Long Day,"* from Norah Jones' first album. Her voice rose and fell with passion and grace, and Hank closed his eyes to let every note sink in.

A young woman sat opposite Paul, playing a banged-up acoustic guitar. Her long black hair cascaded over her shoulders, obscuring her face as she plucked the strings. Her voice swayed between innocent and sultry in a way that suited the song almost perfectly. He stood transfixed, lost in her song.

When she finished the song, she looked up, revealing a face that was wide and plain, but that radiated an angelic sadness. The young woman smiled at Hank as if she had been expecting him.

Her smile broke the spell the music had cast on Hank, and he realized he had been holding his breath.

"Hello, Mr. McCaskill," she said.

"Hello," Hank said, puzzled.

"I don't know if you remember me. I'm Abby Mercer. I'm a friend of Paul's."

"I remember you," Hank said. "I just didn't recognize you. You've lost a lot of weight."

She smiled and nodded. "Paul called me and told me about Sabine. I'm very sorry."

"Thank you."

"I come here to play for patients' families sometimes. Paul is in town, so I thought I'd come over."

"Thank you," he stammered.

"Do you mind if I sing a Christian song?" Abby asked, strumming a few gentle chords.

"Not at all."

Abby pushed her hair back from her face and sang the opening lines of *"Your Love, Oh Lord."*

Hank sat down beside Paul and they both listened. Four songs and fifteen metaphysical minutes later, his reverie was interrupted by the ICU nurse, who asked him to come into the ICU for a moment. Hank's heart sank.

He stepped inside, his heart pounding, expecting to see a sheet draped over his wife. Instead, the nurse motioned to an administrator, who handed him a stack of forms. Hank signed them all without bothering to read them.

Fifteen minutes later, Hank left the ICU to find Paul slumped in a chair again with his eyes closed. Abby was gone. Hank walked downstairs to exit the hospital via the ER entrance, his mind occupied by thoughts of firing bullets into the blue-eyed man's back.

In the ER waiting room, Hank found Abby sitting bundled up in a coat, clutching her guitar case to her chest. She smiled when she saw Hank.

"Mr. McCaskill?"

"Yes?"

"Can I ask a favor?"

"After the way you played, you can ask me almost anything."

"Would you walk me to my car? There were two men standing in the parking lot just now when I went outside. They didn't say anything to me, but they made me feel uneasy. I would have asked Paul, but I didn't want to wake him."

"Sure."

Hank walked outside with Abby right behind him. He scanned the parking lot. Two men stood under a streetlight about a hundred meters from the hospital door, smoking cigarettes and watching the traffic go past. They looked harmless to Hank, but Hank was not a twenty-year-old woman walking alone across a parking lot. The men stopped talking and looked at Hank and Abby.

Hank put his hands in front of him in the ready position, and then remembered that his gun was still at home.

"Are you carrying a gun, Mr. McCaskill?" Abby asked without slowing down.

He looked at her in surprise. "Not right now."

"My Uncle Sean carried a gun most of the time," she replied.

Hank wasn't sure how to take that, so he just walked beside her in silence.

"Thank you, Mr. McCaskill," Abby said as she opened her car door.

"You're welcome, and please call me Hank."

"All right, *Hank*. I just want you to know that everybody at church will be praying for Sabine."

"Thank you."

"You seem to enjoy music."

"That's an understatement," Hank said.

"I'm playing at Riverside Baptist Church tomorrow night if you're interested. You used to go there with Sabine."

"Thanks. I am very much a Christian, but I maintain a healthy skepticism regarding organized religion. I don't go to church much anymore."

"Maybe you should start back."

Hank looked at her warily as she awaited his response. *How can I go to church when all I can think about is killing the man who shot Sabine?*

He regained his composure and said, "Thanks for the invitation. I'll think about it."

13

Near a dilapidated farmhouse east of Charlotte, the blue-eyed man waited beside a locked gate. When a Dodge Caravan pulled up, he glanced inside at the four young men but said nothing. He opened the gate and locked it behind the minivan. A few minutes later, he opened a padlock on the back door of the farmhouse. Inside, he lit oil lamps while the young men whispered and shivered and squirmed.

"Sorry, it's cold in here, but I'll have something to warm you up in a minute."

A few minutes later, he stood in the kitchen, heating water over a butane stove. He listened as the four young men sat shivering and whispering around a worn-out coffee table in the dimly lit living room. When the water boiled, he poured it into a battered but ornate copper teapot that sat on a matching tray beside matching cups.

He placed the tea set on the coffee table and looked at Iqbal.

"How do we know the police won't find us here?" Iqbal asked, his voice was steady, but his eyes darted about and his slender hands trembled.

"Are you worried?" the blue-eyed man asked.

"No, just cautious."

"Trust me, they won't find us here."

"They got Jamal," one of the other young men said. "He might talk."

"Yes, Amal. Jamal got rolled up, but he won't talk."

"We didn't even get that much money, did we?" another of the young men asked.

"No, Daood," the blue-eyed man said. "But y'all *did* learn how to plan an operation. Sometimes things go south, even on a well-planned op. How about I forfeit my share? Deal?"

The blue-eyed man stepped back into the kitchen. Seconds later, he returned and tossed a plastic grocery bag of money onto the coffee table. The young men looked at each other.

Daood sprang up and emptied the bag's contents onto the coffee table. "I'll take my share now," he said, before reaching for a wad of cash.

"Wait a minute, Daood," Amal said. "We count the bills and split the take evenly."

"Slow down, Daood," the blue-eyed man said. "The money isn't going anywhere."

Daood made a sour face but began counting out the bills into four piles.

"I read in the news that you shot that woman at the store," Iqbal said. "Why didn't you tell us?"

"Because I didn't know whether I hit her," the blue-eyed man answered with a shrug.

"I don't want to be involved in killing women," Bilal said. "I want real jihad. There is an American army base just a few miles from the store."

"Yes, and it isn't going anywhere," the blue-eyed man said. "Do you see this tea set? I bought this in Afghanistan." He poured himself a cup of tea and continued. "The man who sold it to me was killed about a month after I bought it. He and one of his sons and one of his daughters died in a drone attack."

The four young men looked at each other and then at the blue-eyed man.

"Right now, you are drinking tea from a set that passed through the hands of Muslim brothers and sisters killed by Americans." His voice assumed a scholarly tone. "They are but three out of tens of thousands. American generals sit in their concrete bunkers and kill Muslims by remote control. Yet you are concerned that a woman - *one woman* - got shot at a store. A store that sells alcohol and pornography. You want real jihad? Real jihad involves collateral damage."

Iqbal studied the contents of his teacup, knotted his brow, and inhaled the aroma. Amal took his teacup, stirred it, and stared into it without drinking. Bilal frowned as he blew into his tea to cool it.

Daood swirled his teacup and sniffed it. "I don't care if she got shot," he said before glancing at the other young men. "As long as we improve our skills and make some money."

"That's the attitude I'm looking for," the blue-eyed man said, glancing at Iqbal and then at Bilal. "Now listen up. I need to go away for a couple of weeks. Don't worry if you don't hear from me and don't sweat it if the police question you. Y'all have solid alibis, so stick with them. Act confused about why you're even being questioned. If you get scared, don't try to hide your fear. Amal, Daood, do *not* ask for a lawyer if you get questioned. If you do, the cops will see that as confirmation that you're involved. You're both still under eighteen and are considered juveniles under the law. You cannot be questioned without an adult present. Answer a few basic questions, like your name and where you live. Then ask if you can leave because you want to have your father present. If they tell you that you can't leave, ask them to call your father so he can serve as a witness. Your father will want to make sure you aren't just being harassed for being Muslim. Iqbal and Bilal, if *you* get questioned, ask the police to call the Pakistani Consulate. That will throw the local cops for a loop. All four of you need to understand that there's no way any cop has enough to hold you. Trust Allah and trust *me*. Got it?"

The other young men nodded, but Iqbal stared into his teacup again and furrowed his brow.

"Our next op will go better," the blue-eyed man said. "You can bet your life on it."

14

"Mr. McCaskill?" a voice asked.

Hank opened his eyes from a dream of sunbeams and silk – a dream in which Sabine was curled up at his side. Instead, she lay on the bed in front of him, her chest rising and falling with each breath. "Yes?"

"You fell asleep in your chair again."

Hank recognized the voice as belonging to a pretty, red-haired ICU nurse who always dressed in bright smocks with teddy bears, Disney characters, or other icons of cheer. Hank found no cheer in her icons.

"I wasn't asleep, I was praying."

"I'm sorry to interrupt your prayer," she said, "but we have a family in the waiting room that would like to visit their grandmother."

"Good night, honey," Hank said to Sabine before rising from his chair and walking out. He wondered if this was the last time he would say good night to his wife.

Abby was sitting in the ER waiting room when Hank walked past on his way out of the hospital.

"Good evening, Mr. McCaskill," she said.

"Hank," he reminded her.

"All right. Hank, could you walk me to my car again tonight?"

"Sure. It's on my way."

"I was hoping to see you at church Sunday night," she said as she picked up her guitar case and followed him out the door.

Abby hummed as she walked beside him, but Hank said nothing. She looked at the spot under the streetlight where the two young men had stood Saturday night. No one was there.

"How is Sabine doing?" she asked.

"She's in a medically induced coma until the swelling goes down."

"How long—" Abby began but Hank's cell phone rang.

"Police," he said to Abby when he saw Ballinger's number. "Hello?"

"Good evening, Major. This is Detective Ballinger. I've got an update on your perp."

"Go ahead."

"Bottom line is, he ain't talking."

"What do you mean? He lawyered up?"

"Yeah, but it's kind of weird. Even though his lawyer was there, he admitted everything, but he ain't giving up his partner."

"Did you interrogate him yourself?"

"I sure did. So did Taggert, and my man Taggert can be pretty persuasive. Thing is, I've rarely seen a perp this stubborn."

"What do you mean, 'stubborn'?"

"Whatever is going on in that criminal mind of his, he's more afraid of his partner than he is of doing four years for armed robbery. He says he'll plead guilty at arraignment and eat the four years."

"Four years? Is that all he's looking at?"

"I'd say he's looking at about 43 months on the armed robbery charge. Knock a couple months off that for good behavior. When I said four years, I was being optimistic."

"I don't believe this," Hank said through clenched teeth. "His partner shot my wife. He threatened Tommy. He tried to kill me. Can't he be charged with *something* more serious?"

"He got a lawyer, and he plans to plead guilty to armed robbery and maybe assault. Maybe. He says you must have shot the place up after you knocked him out. Claims he never fired a shot. Anyway, all he'll ask for is not to be charged with felony murder in case your wife dies."

"Jamal Wilson didn't shoot my wife."

"Yeah, but North Carolina has a felony murder rule. Somebody dies as a result of you committing a felony, and you can be charged with murder. Anyway, the DA here has a full dance card, so a plea to armed robbery is gonna be a no-brainer. He says he won't try to plea bargain anything besides the felony murder charge. Look, Jamal Wilson was unconscious when his partner shot your wife. Even a bored small-town prosecutor wouldn't spend a lot of time on this case."

"I don't believe this."

"Look, I know this doesn't make it any easier for you, Major, but we have other ways of finding the man who shot your wife. Just give us some time."

"Other ways? Like what?"

"I'd rather not say right now," Ballinger replied.

Hank thought about Jamal Wilson serving time. "If Jamal Wilson were going to rat out his boss, seems to me he would have done that during interrogation. Either that or he would plea bargain. That way, he could use his boss's identity as a bargaining chip. I doubt he's going to rat out his boss to one of your informants inside the prison."

Ballinger muttered something unintelligible.

"You still there?" Hank asked.

"I said we have *other ways*, Major. Let's leave it at that. Now, I gotta go, so good night."

Hank hung up and looked around to discover that he was standing beside an empty parking space where Abby's car had been. He waved as she drove away and then spat angrily at the ground. The words "in case your wife dies" echoed in his head as he stumbled toward his hotel room. *The odds of finding the man who shot Sabine just got smaller.*

Hank climbed into bed quietly to avoid waking Paul, who lay asleep on the sofa. A few hours later, he woke from a deep sleep, his heart racing. He bolted upright and looked around. His cell phone was ringing. Hank fumbled with it, turned it upright, and saw that the caller ID was blocked. He answered it anyway.

A familiar, raspy voice replied, "William McCaskill?"

Hank felt a sensation like being immersed in cold water as he fought the urge to respond. Instead, he just listened. No background sounds, no breathing. Only a trace of a Southern accent. Hank said nothing, in hopes that the caller would speak again, but after a few seconds, the caller hung up.

I know that voice. It's like a fingerprint. He started dialing Detective Ballinger's number when the clock beside the bed caught his eye.

"Four twenty-two," he said aloud, "which would make me a first-rate jerk of a witness." He hung up and stared resentfully at the ceiling. He glanced at the sofa where Paul had slept, and then around the room. Paul was gone. Hank shook his head, slapped the pillow, and grunted. He thought about trying to go back to sleep but hauled himself out of bed. After pulling on the clothes he had worn the previous day, he trotted downstairs, where his weather-beaten Toyota 4x4 was parked under a lamppost.

Tommy was opening the register when Hank drove up at nine minutes after five. Tommy looked around warily as the headlights played off the front of the store, but he smiled when Hank climbed out of the truck. Hank clenched his fists as he glanced at the spot where Sabine's Escape had been parked when she was shot, but, for Tommy's sake, he forced a smile as he walked inside.

"Morning, Tommy. I didn't know if you'd be working this morning, but I figured I'd come by. Coffee smells good."

"Just brewed it."

Hank walked down the aisle where the robber's bullets had scattered the bottles of cold medicine and noticed a faint purple stain on one shelf. He glanced at the beer cooler. The glass had already been replaced, as had the glass on the store front. Hank then forced himself to focus his thoughts on the coffee. He poured himself a cup while Tommy counted coins into the register. Tommy's hands shook as he counted.

"Are you all right, Tommy?"

"Yeah, but the boss moved me back to the morning shift. Said it would be better for security. How's your wife?"

"Still in the hospital."

"I'm sorry, Hank," Tommy said. He shuddered and did not look up from the register.

"Yeah, me too. But mostly I'm sorry I wasn't carrying my pistol when the place got held up. I thought they were going to shoot you."

Tommy looked up abruptly. "That guy you took down, he scared me. Actually, they both scared me, but in different ways."

"Did you think it was odd that the robber knew your name?"

Tommy looked around the store and then down at the register drawer. "Yeah."

"What's wrong?"

"A man's got to make a living, you know. This job ain't much, but I get insurance for me and my mom. Most convenience stores don't do much for you when it comes to benefits."

"Understood. Did you tell the detective that the robber called you by name?"

Tommy nodded and looked around again. "But when I went down to the station to review my statement, I changed it. I told him I didn't remember much about what happened."

"What?"

"Look, Hank, I'm scared, okay? The morning after we got robbed, that blue-eyed man called my house. He said, 'Next time you talk to the police, you don't remember much of anything.' Then he told me my home address, what clothes my mom had worn the day before and the name of the school where my ex-wife sends our little boy. He even described Thomas's book bag. It has a yellow dinosaur on the back."

"Are you sure it was the guy who robbed the store?"

"Positive," Tommy said. "I'd recognize that voice anywhere." He shivered and then shoved the register drawer shut. "I'm scared to come to work, and I'm scared to stay home." He looked up at Hank. "I'm scared for my mother, and I'm scared for my son."

"Do you have caller ID? Did you get his number?"

"It was blocked."

Hank glanced in the direction the tall man had fled. *I really should have shot him.*

An hour and a half after his conversation with Tommy, Hank and Paul were eating breakfast at Pete's.

"Where were you this morning at about four-thirty?" Hank asked.

Paul flashed a wolfish grin at Hank. "I went for a run."

Hank frowned as he watched his son methodically dissect a pile of hash browns drenched in ketchup and hot sauce. Hank toyed with the steak and eggs on his plate and then looked up. Pete sat engrossed in a pile of paperwork at a table in the corner. Hank stabbed the steak with his fork and held it up to examine it in the light.

"Is something wrong with your steak, Hank?" Pete asked. Hank looked up to see Pete staring at him.

"No, the steak's fine."

Paul scooted over as Pete slid onto the bench opposite Hank.

"Do the windows look clean? I just hired a new guy to do my windows."

"The windows are almost spotless. I was just thinking about the man who shot Sabine."

"Maybe you should think about your breakfast instead, amigo."

"Right. Pete, you've been in business here for about six years?"

"Just over seven. Time flies when you're out of the game."

"It does. You ever seen anybody doing recon on your place?"

"Naw." Pete shook his head. "I know how to spot somebody doing recon."

"I know you do."

Pete propped his meaty elbows on the table, leaned forward, and lowered his voice. "There's a cop named Murray comes in here a couple of times a week. He's good. I tell him anything suspicious that I've noticed, mostly just tweakers and drunks, though. An occasional gang banger. No recon, no armed robbers."

"The guy I'm thinking about is not a tweaker, and he's not your average armed robber."

"I have security cameras, and I carry. So does Kathleen. She runs the beauty shop next door. So does Dewey over at the tire store."

"I wish all it took was cameras and guns, but this guy does his homework. He'll hit when your place is nearly empty. He will disable your security cameras, and he won't hesitate to shoot first if you're carrying."

"How do you know so much about him?"

"Gut feeling."

On the way to the airport, Paul asked Hank to drive past the store where Sabine was shot. Hank agreed. Paul's green eyes narrowed in concentration as Hank slowed his truck in front of the store.

"So, this is the place?" Paul asked. He looked across the street at the wooded lot. "And that's where he ran afterwards?"

"Yeah. I can't drive past here anymore without thinking about it."

After dropping Paul off at the airport, Hank knelt at Sabine's bedside in silent prayer. He could sense the eyes of the ICU nurse on his back, but he didn't care. When he opened his eyes and stood, the pretty, red-haired nurse from his previous visit stood beside him. Hank expected her to tell him to leave. Instead, she just smiled.

"Good morning, Mr. McCaskill."

"I'm sorry if I overstayed my welcome—"

"No, you're welcome to stay as long as we don't have too many patients and visitors at one time."

Hank extended his hand. "Please call me Hank."

"All right, Hank. My name is Samantha. Look, I know this is very personal, but maybe you should try talking to your wife. Comatose patients often benefit from hearing the voices of people they love."

"Thanks. I should have already been doing that."

Hank sat by Sabine's bedside and took her hand. Although Samantha was out of earshot, he spoke in a whisper. "Paul flies back to Fort Campbell this morning, honey."

He looked toward the nurse's desk and cleared his throat. "I wish you could see Paul. He didn't have much to say, but he looks good. Strong as an oak tree. Michael went back to Camp Lejeune on Sunday. He's going to be very busy this week getting ready for an amphibious exercise. Joseph flew back to Nicaragua Monday night, but he'll come home again for Christmas. Says the mission needs him. He's got calloused hands and a deep suntan. Paul and I got your car back from the police lot today. Detective Ballinger even had it cleaned before I picked it up."

He listened to the whirring and beeping of the machinery that surrounded his wife. He thought about the bloodstains that must have been on the seat and carpet of the Escape.

"You've been here for five days, Sabine," he said, his voice shaking. "If you're dreaming, I hope you're dreaming about our honeymoon and the life ahead of us, but whatever you're dreaming about, I'm ready for you to wake up."

15

Hank's days devolved into a routine of eating takeout food, sleeping in the hotel room, waiting for Sabine to regain consciousness, and reciting information about her condition on the phone. Her mother was in poor health and could not leave Germany. Most of Hank's relatives lived in Georgia or Alabama, which was too far for them to travel, although Hank had often driven to visit them when he was on leave from the Army. Several people from the church called to say they were praying for Sabine, and someone from the church came by the hospital daily. Promises of prayer poured in, as did get well cards, but few people visited Hank. Even fewer offered any real help. Upton, Chapman, Decker, Litton, and Davis, however, kept the yard up. Miss Helen from church had a key to Hank's house, and she came by to tidy up and leave an occasional casserole, but Hank never saw her because she came by only when he was away. Hank felt almost completely alone.

In the thirteen days since Sabine had been shot, she had not regained consciousness, but she had begun moving her fingers and her lung function was improving. Because he no longer needed to stay close to the hospital, Hank checked out of the hotel and began driving from his house daily to see Sabine.

In the early afternoon, he drove to Dr. Chan's office in a medical center near the hospital. Although he hoped for some good news, a sense of dread came over him as he walked into the waiting room.

Dr. Chan was smiling when she welcomed him into her office, but as soon as she shut the door, her expression transformed into a stoic mask, a mask formed by long years of delivering tragic news. Hank had worn that face on occasion as an army officer.

She sat behind a sterile gray desk and motioned for Hank to sit. "Does Sabrina have a living will?" she asked.

Hank swallowed hard. "Her name is *Sabine*, it's a very common German name, and *Sabine* does not have living will. Why is my wife still unconscious?"

Dr. Chan glanced at the chart on her desk.

"Your wife is not just unconscious, she is in a medically induced coma. According to the ultrasound and imaging, her aorta does not appear to be torn. I can also tell you that her heart muscle is healing from the injuries she sustained as the bullet passed through her chest. And the fluid that accumulated around her lungs is being reabsorbed. All of that is good news. The bad news is that her body is not responding to our efforts to bring her out of that coma. Some patients never regain consciousness from medically induced comas. I'm afraid Sabine may be one of those."

"And she may not."

"I understand that this might not be the best time to discuss terminal care issues, but, in my experience, there is no good time."

"No, Dr. Chan," Hank said, "we are not going to talk about terminal care issues. Not now, not ever. We are going to talk about getting Sabine out of this coma."

"I know this is difficult for you, but you have to start thinking about what you're going to do if she doesn't recover."

"Doesn't recover? By when?"

"Based on broad statistical studies, comatose patients who don't recover within a few weeks are unlikely to recover at all. If she suffered brain damage and remains unconscious for over a month, she will be considered to be in a persistent vegetative state. That has legal ramifications. Of course, *there are* miracle stories about patients being in such a state for months and then suddenly waking, but those stories are statistical anomalies. The longer she stays comatose, the more likely it is that she'll never recover. Lung infections are the most common cause of mortality in cases like this, and with the fluid—"

"Are you working your way up to asking me when I want to pull the plug?" Hank asked through clenched teeth. "She's only been here for two weeks!"

"Mr. McCaskill, your wife's body is simply not responding. She is still on a respirator and still unconscious. No one will push you to make a decision until you're ready, but you need to start thinking about this now."

Hank was unable to speak and was barely able to think. Instead of responding, he found himself immersed in a memory of sitting beside Sabine on the back porch, talking about their future together. He said nothing as he rose and walked out.

That night, Abby was waiting for Hank in the ER waiting room. When she saw him, she stood and smiled.

"How is Sabine?" she asked. He looked at her and tried to speak, but his mind was replaying the moment when he had found Sabine slumped over the wheel. Lost in a fantasy of shooting the blue-eyed man, Hank stumbled into a potted plant. He muttered a curse and then sat and muttered a prayer.

Abby said nothing as she took her guitar out of the case and strummed a few chords. Hank could not identify the tune, so he just sat, his face in his hands, lost in the sounds of the chords resonating through the empty room. Eventually, he looked up. "She may not make it."

"Are you okay?" she asked.

Hank nodded, stood, and walked outside with Abby at his side. Once again, two men stood under the streetlight, smoking. Abby stepped a little closer to him, but said nothing until they reached her car.

"Thank you for walking me to my car," Abby said, her gaze fixed on the two men. "At school they have volunteer escorts so students don't have to walk across campus alone late at night."

"So, you're in school here?" he blurted out.

"Yeah, I'm a music major at Methodist University. You like music, don't you?"

"That's an understatement."

"What kind?"

"Hmm?" Hank asked.

"What kind of music do you like best?"

"Oh, I don't know. I guess I'd choose the singer-songwriters of the early '70s if I had to choose a single genre."

"You'd get along with my Aunt Melissa. That's what she listens to."

"Thank you," Hank said.

"For what?"

"For playing for me tonight."

"I enjoy playing for an attentive audience."

Hank had the disturbing feeling that he had just awakened. He realized that he and Abby were standing by her car, and he had no sense of how long they had been standing there. Abby put her guitar case in the passenger seat but did not get in.

"Are you all right?" she asked.

"Do your parents live in Fayetteville?" Hank asked.

"No, but I was raised by my Aunt Melissa. I grew up here, and now I'm going to school here at Methodist."

"From Fayetteville, huh? Was your dad in the Army?"

"No, my Uncle Sean, Aunt Melissa's husband, was like a father to me. He was a cop."

"Your uncle was a cop. That explains a few things."

"Paul never talks about what you did in the Army, so, um what did you do?" Abby asked.

"Whatever needed to be done. Intelligence work, mostly."

"That sounds exciting."

"It wasn't," he said. "I fought the war on terror one map and one spreadsheet at a time. I led small teams that sifted through mountains of reports looking for specks of gold. Being an intelligence analyst isn't nearly as exciting as being a musician."

"Being a musician isn't all that exciting most of the time. But since you like music, do you want to come to church to hear me play?"

"I appreciate the offer, but, like I said before, I'm not much of a churchgoer. Thank you, though."

"All right, then. I won't ask you to come to church again."

"You played beautifully tonight."

"You always say that, but thank you. Are you sure you're okay?"

They stood in silence in the chilly air.

"When did you decide to make music your profession?" he asked, surprising himself almost as much as he surprised her.

"Oh, wow. My Aunt Melissa was a piano teacher, and she was a good one. She started teaching me when I was five. I fell in love with music from the moment I learned to play *'Twinkle, twinkle.'*"

"So, music is your childhood sweetheart?"

"Still is. I never really thought about doing anything else."

"Interesting," Hank said.

"When did you know you wanted to be a soldier?" she asked.

"Oh, I can't pin down a date, but from the time I was in grade school, I liked to play army. I just sort of fell into it naturally, without a lot of rational thought. God put it in my heart to be a soldier, and that's what I became. Funny thing is, I hate war."

"Sounds like my Uncle Sean," Abby said, smiling. "He never wanted to do anything else but be a cop, but sometimes he hated the situations he got put into. You remind me of him."

Hank felt uneasy being compared to her uncle, but he smiled. "I just hope your Uncle Sean is taller and better looking than me. And I hope he doesn't mind being compared to a grumpy middle-aged man."

"Oh, I don't think he'd mind."

Abby glanced at her guitar case and then into the distance.

"Getting late," Hank said. "I'd better get going."

"Hank, since you won't come to see me play at church, you could come see me play somewhere else. I also play in a band. We're playing Saturday night at 'The Steam Room.' It's that new coffee shop downtown."

"What kind of music do y'all play?"

"Screamo death metal."

Hank raised his eyebrows. "Screamo death metal?"

"Yeah. Screamo death metal."

"I think I'll pass, Abby."

"Aw, you should come, Hank. Paul wanted to come, but he's on a training exercise."

"I'll check my calendar."

"It might do you good."

"Tell you what, it's been a long time since I've heard live music. I'll come to see you play Saturday night."

"Awesome!" Abby exclaimed, her face beaming as she climbed into her car. "You're a good man, Hank."

Again, Hank had no sense of how much time had passed, but he found himself waving as Abby drove away. When her taillights were out of sight, Hank climbed into his truck. Instead of driving home, he sat there with the engine running.

"I'm a good man, huh?" he muttered. "What would you know?"

He pushed a CD into the player and listened for six minutes and twenty-two seconds until the dying notes of the Flying Burrito Brothers' *"Wild Horses"* faded into the night.

When Hank got home, he picked up the mail, separated the get-well cards from the bills, and glanced at the photos in the foyer on his way to the kitchen table. He tossed the bills on top of a two-inch pile of un-opened mail and opened the refrigerator to find some sort of casserole dish on the main shelf. *Miss Helen has been by.* He filled a coffee cup with cold water and sipped it while rubbing his temples. *I'd rather be drinking something stronger.* He played the lone message on the voice mail.

"Hank, this is Pete. I thought about what you said this morning, and I'm pretty sure I know what you have in mind. We think alike, especially when it comes to fishing. If you need any help planning your big trip, just give me a call."

Hank thought about Pete's message as he poised his finger over the call-back button. Just then, his cell phone rang. Detective Ballinger's number showed in the caller ID.

"Talk to me."

"Major, this is Detective Ballinger."

"Good to hear from you."

"How is your wife doing?"

"Still comatose. The doctor asked me about taking her off the respirator."

Ballinger exhaled through his teeth. "I'm sorry."

"So, have you identified the man who shot her?"

"No, but we're still working on it. What I called about was to tell you that Jamal Wilson got himself iced."

"What?"

"I said Jamal Wilson got himself killed."

Hank set his cup down. "How?"

"Happened yesterday at Caledonia State Pen up in Tillery. He was working in the cannery, and someone stuck him in the kidney with a ten-inch shank. Guard said it looked like they made it out of one of those big kitchen spoons. Shoved it all the way in, from what I hear."

"What for?" Hank asked.

"Caledonia's where they house a lot of lifers, so who knows? He was still fresh meat. Hadn't even been there a week."

"You said, 'cannery.' They have a cannery in the prison?"

"Yeah. Caledonia is a prison farm. They grow tomatoes and stuff."

"Tomatoes, huh?" Hank asked. "The prison guards should have some idea who shanked him."

"If they do, they haven't told us. Look, murders happen in the big house sometimes. Maybe he stole somebody's smokes. Could have been some sort of gang thing. You never know."

"Then again, maybe somebody didn't want him to say anything that would lead us to the man who shot Sabine."

"I wouldn't go jumping to conclusions," Ballinger said.

"Have they made an arrest yet?"

"No."

"Come on. There can't be that many people — inmates — who were in the cannery when he got killed."

"I'll keep you posted. But lifers ain't got much to lose, so sometimes they kill somebody as a favor. You know, for a friend or relative. Something like that."

"Yeah. Something like that," Hank said. He thought about telling Ballinger that the blue-eyed man had called him and Tommy to intimidate them, but something in the back of his mind told him not to.

"You still there?" Ballinger asked.

"Yeah. I was just thinking."

"About what?"

"Dead criminals. Thanks for the phone call."

As Hank hung up the phone, uneasiness burned in his chest. *I should have seen this coming.*

Hank sat in his recliner, lost in thought, his hands clasped in front of him as if he were praying. After a few moments, he rose and dialed Michael's number.

"Good evening, Lieutenant McCaskill," Hank said with artificial cheer.

"Is there a change in Mom's condition?"

"No, son, I just called because I need a favor."

"*You* need a favor? So, is this role-reversal night?"

"No, son, by my calendar it's just an ordinary Tuesday evening."

"Dad, I don't mean to be abrupt, but I was already in bed. It's almost 2200, and I have to run ten kilometers with the battalion commander tomorrow morning."

"Think back to all the times when you were a teenager and your mom and I waited up for you to come home."

"All right. What do you need?"

"You remember Chuck Anderson that you went to high school with?"

"Yeah."

"Does Chuck's dad still work as a prison guard?"

"Yes, but the term is 'corrections officer,' not 'prison guard.' So, what's this about?"

"It's about running down a lead."

"Please don't go playing cop, Dad."

"Get me Alan Anderson's number, and I'll think about it. By the way, the term is 'police officer,' not 'cop.'"

When Hank called Alan Anderson, it was almost eleven.

"I'm sorry for calling so late," he began, but Alan interrupted.

"No worries. I'm sorry about what happened to Sabine. I know we haven't seen each other since our boys graduated, but I'll help you with anything you need."

"That's what I'm calling about, Alan. I want to find out about the accomplice of the man who shot Sabine."

"What about him?"

"His name is Jamal Wilson. He's dead. He had just been transferred to Caledonia prison farm in Tillery, and somebody shanked him."

"You don't say. What's the story?"

Hank told him everything that Detective Ballinger had related.

"Well, it must have just happened," Alan said. "I haven't heard anything about it."

"Could you look into this and see what's going on? The murder, the investigation, what this guy was into. I'm sure the Bureau of Prisons will publish some sort of report."

"Yeah, but the report won't be out for a while, and they'll be tight-lipped while the investigation is in progress. I'll see what I can find out through the rumor mill and call you back on Saturday. Somebody's going to know something about it. In prison, the walls have ears."

16

Hank looked at the full-length mirror that hung behind the door of the master bedroom and scowled. He focused on the drooping breast pocket of his plaid flannel shirt, and then on his Wrangler jeans, whose seams were worn nearly white. His eyes fell to his scuffed brown loafers. *I look like a throwback to the 1980s.* After years of having the Army dictate his wardrobe, his closet held a bewildering assortment of shirts and slacks and shoes from three different decades. *I am not going out in faded jeans and a scuffed-up pair of shoes.*

He reached into his closet and retrieved a pair of gray polyester slacks and a green knit shirt. He tossed the shirt into the dryer and ironed the slacks, only to find that the waistline was three inches too large. Then he scoured the shoe shelf and found a pair of black wingtips he had forgotten he owned. A dark blue jacket hung on the left of his closet. He pulled the jacket off the hanger and knocked the dust off the shoulders. For an instant, Hank thought he smelled Sabine's perfume, and a mental image of her lying comatose in the hospital passed before his mind's eye. *They call it a ghost when you sensed the presence of a person who's dead, but what do they call it when you sensed the absence of someone who is still alive?* A car horn in his driveway interrupted his thoughts. Hank pulled the bedroom curtains aside to see Pete's car idling out front and then bounded downstairs.

"Thanks for driving."

"No problem. I don't drive as much since Cindy passed away. All I do is work, watch TV, and go fishing. I'm pretty sure I've read *Clear and Present Danger* about nine times."

"You carrying?"

"Oh yeah," Pete said. "I'm not just the designated driver tonight, I'm the designated shooter. No booze for me."

Twenty minutes later, Pete and Hank joined a small crowd waiting outside an old brick building in the historic district. A sign depicting a steaming cup of coffee identified the building as 'The Steam Room,' and a poster in front read, 'Abby and the Blue Crew.' The poster sported dark blue and burnt orange silhouettes, with fonts reminiscent of advertisements from the 1970s.

The crowd slowly transformed into a line, and Hank and Pete filed inside. Pete got a table while Hank worked his way up to a wood and glass counter that sat atop a Depression-era floor of black and white tile. The large squares reminded Hank of a chessboard. Small tables arranged in rows resembled chess pieces. A few dozen people chatted in an open room beyond the counter, and a dark-haired woman, about eight months pregnant, looked across the counter at Hank.

"What can I get you, sir?"

Hank looked through the glass at the selection of beers. A can of Pabst Blue Ribbon looked out of place among the microbrews with strange names and cartoonish labels. His eyes lingered on a bottle of Blue Moon and then drifted back to the can of PBR. Hank wondered what Madison would think of her future father-in-law drinking a PBR. "One Blue Moon and one club soda."

About forty people were seated at tables around the stage, which was a raised floor with lighter colored flooring. Hank and Pete squeezed into a tiny booth beside the wall, where Hank sipped his Blue Moon and watched the stage. Pete peered over his club soda at the door. Abby hummed as she adjusted her guitar, the same old acoustic she had played in the hospital. Behind her stood a skinny young man tuning an electric bass and a rotund, bearded man tinkering with a snare drum. The bass player and the drummer were talking, but Hank could not make out their words. Abby looked up at the crowd occasionally and smiled, but she showed no sign of recognizing Hank. She glanced at the door and then at an empty stool to her right.

"The place is packed," Pete said.

Hank nodded.

"You don't have much to say, Hank. What's up?"

"I don't like crowds," Hank said.

"You haven't changed much, amigo. Relax. I got your six."

Hank turned his attention to the people around him. Immediately to his left stood a muscular man in his thirties who sported a bushy beard. The man wore a flannel shirt and faded jeans and held a PBR can. Hank's eyes drifted down to the man's feet. He wore leather work boots. Hank then scanned the room from left to right. Seven of the men in the audience were dressed the same. He took a long drink of his Blue Moon and glanced down at his black wingtips.

"Pete, does it seem odd to you that some of these guys are dressed like you and me back in the eighties?"

"Not at all," Pete replied. "We were trendsetters."

Hank chuckled and looked up to see a young man walking onstage, carrying an electric guitar.

"About time you got here," Abby said, as much to the crowd as to the young man. A few people in the audience chuckled as the man took out his guitar and sat on the stool to Abby's right.

"I'm Abby, and this is my friend, Ty. To my left, we've got Tom and Jerry on the bass and drums."

The drummer hit a tat-tat-tat-boom and a few in the audience chuckled.

"Their names really are Tom and Jerry, by the way. No joke. Anyway, we're going to play a few songs for y'all tonight, most of them old songs."

A few people clapped as a skinny young man approached the stage, cupping something in his hands. He stood stiffly at the mic to Abby's left.

"Our friend Jared is going to join us on this first one with his harmonica. You know, it's really nice playing for people who like classic rock."

"Don't that little girl make you feel old?" Pete asked.

"I didn't need *her* to make me feel old," Hank said.

As a few people chuckled, Abby and the band started playing. Hank recognized the song as Neil Young's "Heart of Gold." At first, Jared's harmonica sounded wheezy, and Abby's vocals were weak. By the first chorus of the song, however, Abby had relaxed, and her voice rang out as sweetly as it had the first night Hank had heard her sing. He turned to look at two young women in the audience who were singing along. As he watched them, his heartbeat seemed to slow until it beat in time with the drummer's insistent, pulse-like drumming. The familiar melody brought him an unexpected peace. He closed his eyes and found himself immersed in a memory of swimming in blood-warm waters fringed by sugar-white sand. A tropical sun simmered overhead, and Sabine swam at his side.

A sudden popping sound from an amp jarred Hank from his reverie. He reached for his pistol, but his fingers grasped only the fabric of his slacks. His gun was at home, locked in the safe. He inhaled, closed his eyes again, tried to control his heartbeat, and began singing along with Abby, so softly that only Pete could hear. Hank was immersed again in a pleasant memory, but he opened his eyes just as Abby sang the closing words.

"Thank y'all," Abby said as the last echoes of the song faded away, her southern accent more distinct than usual. The audience clapped, except for a bearded middle-aged man in a Lynyrd Skynyrd tee shirt. He stood and shouted, "Oh yeah!"

Hank clapped a little longer and a little louder than anyone else but stopped and grabbed his beer when a nearby couple glanced his way.

"This next one is from the 1972 album '*Eat a Peach*' by the Allman Brothers, which was the first album the Allman Brothers released after the death of Duane Allman," Abby said. "It's called 'Melissa,' but it's sometimes called 'Sweet Melissa' because—" Abby stopped and looked right at Hank. She waved and smiled. Half the audience turned and looked at Hank. "This next one goes out to my friend Hank, over there." She pointed at Pete and Hank's table. "He and his friend look like tough guys, but they're a couple of teddy bears. Hank, honey, this one's for you."

Pete patted Hank on the shoulder. Hank squirmed, pulled his beer in close, and scanned the people in the room, looking for concealed weapons or hostile body language. He looked toward the stage as Abby and Ty played their guitars in a soothing harmony. Abby's voice captivated Hank with the song's first word.

Once again, Hank closed his eyes and immersed himself in a familiar melody. At first, he thought it strange for a woman to be singing "*Melissa*," but as he listened, it occurred to him that the song was about a perfect love, sung in third person. It also occurred to him that not many love songs were sung in third person. Maybe there should be more songs like that. When Abby got to the lines that asked whether the crossroads would ever let him go, a crushing grief seized Hank and he found himself unable to sing, barely able even to breathe.

He stood, fought off dizziness, and finished his beer as he threaded his way through the crowd to the counter. Hank glanced behind him to see Ty plucking and bending the strings of his guitar in a lead that resonated with passion and intensity. Abby and the Blue Crew did not sound like amateurs at a coffee shop. They sounded like a young band almost ready to release their own material. The crowd erupted in applause when the song ended.

Hank bought a can of PBR and another club soda for Pete. He returned to the table during a pause between songs to find Abby drinking from a coffee cup and Ty tuning his guitar.

"Do you think it's odd that so many young people like this old music?" Hank asked.

Pete laughed. "You ever listen to the stuff on the radio these days?"

Before Hank could reply, Abby leaned toward the microphone. "Jared is going to join us again, because this song really needs a flute to set it off just right."

Jared approached the stage again, this time carrying a flute instead of a harmonica. Seconds later, Abby and Ty played the opening chords of Justin Hayward's "Forever Autumn." Hank drained half of his beer in one gulp and listened. Jared's flute added a second voice to the song, a wordless voice that spoke to Hank in the pure language of the heart. Again, a sudden, crushing grief seized Hank. After a moment, he recovered and managed to sit stoically through the rest of the song, his hand tight on his beer. Some of the words burned into his mind, like the voice of the man who had shot Sabine, but he endured the song's melancholy lyrics without making any sounds or facial expressions. By the time the song ended, Hank had crushed his PBR can.

Hank sat through the rest of the concert in a daze, not entirely because of the three more cans of PBR he drank. When the music ended, he found himself sitting alone at the tiny table, his head spinning from too much beer. Pete was chatting with someone Hank didn't know, while the band members helped Jerry disassemble his drum kit. Abby was mingling with the audience.

Hank stood as she walked to his table. "Nice work, young lady."

"Did you enjoy it?" she asked.

"Enjoy it? Abby, that was beautiful. And you didn't play any 'screamo death metal.'"

"No," she confessed with a twinkle in her eye, "we didn't. That was a joke. We don't do screamo death metal. We cover classic rock songs. And we're working on three songs of our own."

"I see," Hank said. "A joke."

"Yeah. And you fell for it."

"Yes, I did."

Abby's eyes lit up, causing Hank to worry that she was looking at him, but then someone stepped up behind him.

"Hank, this is my boyfriend, Brandon," Abby said.

Hank turned around to face a wall of red plaid flannel. He looked up, up and then up some more until he made eye contact with a young man at least six inches taller than himself, a man with a toothy grin and the shoulders of a linebacker. When the young man extended a meaty hand downward toward him, Hank shook it, and was relieved to come away with no broken bones.

"Brandon Nowak," the young man said.

"Hank McCaskill. I'm an old friend of Abby's, and I mean 'old' literally."

"Abby has told me a lot about you," Brandon said.

"The stuff she said, was it good or was it true?" Hank asked, raising an eyebrow.

Brandon looked puzzled. "She didn't say anything bad about you, sir. She said you're a retired major."

"I retired about a month ago," he said, noting that two attempts at humor had fallen flat.

"How many years were you enlisted?"

"How did you know I was enlisted?"

"Your age. You must have had enlisted time."

"Yeah, thirteen years of enlisted time. Don't ask me why I waited so long."

"I won't," Brandon said. "Are you enjoying retired life, sir?"

"I don't know yet," Hank answered. "I don't feel like a retiree. My wife is in the hospital in a coma. I feel... stuck between two lives."

"I'm sorry about her getting shot," Brandon said. "Abby told me about it."

Brandon's reminder of Sabine's getting shot stung Hank, and he realized he had said too much for an introduction. "I'm sure she'll get better. It's just going to take time. So, what do you do in the Army?"

"I'm a combat medic."

"Good for you. You know, I nearly enlisted as a medic, but for some reason, I wanted to do intelligence work."

"I'm a medic now, but I plan to get out in a couple of years and go to college."

"Sounds like a good career plan. What do you want to major in?"

"Pre-med, then medical school."

"Medical school, huh?"

"Yes, sir. Most likely emergency medicine. What about you? What are you going to do now that you're retired?"

"Me? I'm going to grow tomatoes," Hank said and then looked off into the distance. The monster in his chest was threatening to rise again. He sensed that Brandon was puzzled, but before Brandon said anything, Abby interrupted.

"Brandon, could you help Tom and Jerry load the van?" she asked.

"Sure. It was nice meeting you, sir," Brandon said, reaching down for Hank's hand. "And if you need help with anything, let me know. I appreciate your looking out for Abby at the hospital." He walked toward the stage where Ty was coiling a cable.

"So, do you like him?" Abby asked. She sat down on the edge of a chair and motioned for Hank to sit down.

Hank took a wobbly step toward the chair but remained standing. "I think he's a keeper," he said at last. Abby's invitation hadn't been about the music. He glanced at Brandon, who picked up a bass amp with four thick fingers. "He's got good manners and seems to have a good head on his shoulders. Even has good teeth."

"Yeah, he's hot," she said, smiling and looking at Brandon as he carried the amp toward the back door. "My roommate says he looks like Channing Tatum, but blond."

Hank nodded as if he knew who that was. "Abby, if I wanted to describe that young man with just one adjective, I'd choose 'large,' and if I were allocated a second adjective, I'd pick 'polite.'"

Abby giggled. Then she clasped Hank's shoulder and stood up. "I knew you'd like him."

"You were right. I *do* like him."

"Bye, Hank. Thanks for coming tonight."

"Thanks for inviting me. I enjoyed it."

As Abby and Brandon walked away, Brandon draped a log-like arm over her shoulders. Hank thought back to the day at Pete's when Sabine had said that Michael and Madison reminded her of herself and Hank. Now he understood. As he watched Brandon and Abby step through the back door and into the night, he thought about Sabine lying in her hospital bed. Hank stood, thought about ordering another beer, but ordered a black coffee to go instead. He flagged down Pete, who was saying goodbye to a young couple.

"Pete, can you drop me at the Cape Fear Valley Hospital?"

Pete threw a muscular arm around Hank's shoulders. "On one condition, amigo. You tell Sabine that she needs to come with us next time."

17

An hour later, after visiting Sabine and again begging God to let her wake up, Hank took a cab back home. As the front door closed behind him, the monster in his chest threatened to rise again.

Although he had already had several beers, he poured himself two fingers of Glenmorangie and studied the glass in the lamplight. He poured two more fingers and then raised the glass to his lips. After pausing to inhale the rich aroma, his lips touched the sweet, sweet fire. The liquor rolled across his tongue with that old familiar burn. As the whiskey hit Hank's stomach, the silence of his empty house closed about him like a dark curtain, but the raspy voice of the blue-eyed man mocked him in his mind. The whiskey helped suppress the monster in his chest, but it did not silence that voice.

With Jamal Wilson's death, the police were one step further from finding the owner of that voice. He indulged in a momentary fantasy of drowning the blue-eyed man, holding him underwater — so he could not speak — and watching his face turn blue. Hank caught himself almost immediately and took a deep breath. He needed to focus on something besides revenge. He drained his glass and poured another two-finger glass, longing for the dreamless slumber that whiskey could bring. His mind kept chugging along despite the alcohol.

The only obvious link to the man who shot Sabine was now broken, but surely there were less obvious links. The police just had to find them. He looked above the mantel to a photograph of himself and Sabine, taken not long after they had met. Twenty-eight years had gone by much too quickly. He remembered how, on the night she had been shot, Sabine had warned him against drinking too much. Hank sipped his whiskey and said aloud, "God, turn my thoughts to you. Bring me peace and help me find the man who did this."

As soon as Hank had spoken, however, he wondered if God would answer a prayer born of a desire for vengeance and uttered by a drunk man. He looked at the bottle of Scotch, which held enough Glenmorangie for one more four-finger glass. Instead of pouring another glass, he took the bottle to the kitchen and held it over the sink, hesitating as he thought about how much it had cost. Before he could decide what to do, his cell phone rang. He put the bottle down and answered, although he did not recognize the number.

"Talk to me."

"Hank, this is Alan Anderson. I'm sorry for calling so late, but, um, are you sitting down?"

"Yeah," Hank said, casting a guilty glance behind him at his empty recliner. "Why?"

"There's something strange going on with this case."

"I think so too. It just seemed strange that Jamal Wilson got shanked in the cannery."

"Well, that's what's strange, Hank. He didn't get shanked in the cannery."

"Let me guess, he got clubbed with a lead pipe in the library."

"What are you talking about?"

"Never mind. What happened? Where did he get shanked?"

"He didn't get shanked at all. That's what I'm trying to tell you. He got shot."

Hank felt his pulse quicken. "Say that again."

"He got shot. He was out working on the prison farm, and somebody shot him with a large-caliber rifle from a distance. A sheriff's deputy found a hide site over five hundred yards from where Jamal Wilson was working."

"Shot. Large-caliber rifle. Hide site. Five hundred yards," Hank said. He walked over to his recliner and collapsed into it, his head spinning as much from the news as from the beer and the Scotch.

Not many people have the skills to shoot accurately at that distance from a concealed location, Hank thought. He's not necessarily a sniper, but he's military, law enforcement, or a serious hunter. And he would have needed a good rifle and optics — and probably an inside source — to positively identify his target.

"What was the wind speed the day Jamal Wilson was shot?" Hank asked.

"Wind speed? How should I know?"

"Sorry about that, Alan. It was a dumb question."

"Yeah. Anyway, there's something strange going on with this case. I don't know why that detective told you the kid got shanked, but the ground truth is Jamal Wilson was shot. I don't know what's going on here, but I'd rather not dig any deeper."

"Understood. Thank you, Alan. You've already helped, far more than you know. Please tell your family I said hello."

Hank hung up, rose from the recliner, and fetched a can of club soda. Although he wanted a beer, or, better yet, another glass of Glenmorangie, he drained the club soda in three gulps. and collapsed into his recliner again.

"Curiouser and curiouser," he said to the ceiling. Why would Ballinger lie? Hank crushed the empty can in his hand and stared at the crinkled metal.

Hank rose, fetched Sabine's address book from a kitchen drawer, opened it to the middle, and flipped to the name "JD and Kelly Mc-Caskill." He punched in the number and listened as the voice mail picked up. Somewhat relieved, Hank said, "JD, this is your brother Hank—"

Someone picked up. "Hank? It's good to hear from you."

"I hope I didn't call at a bad time, JD."

"There's never a bad time to call your big brother."

"Well, it's been a while since we talked, and I didn't know—"

"Joseph told me all about Sabine," JD said. "I would have called sooner, but I didn't know if you'd want to talk to me."

"I would have talked to you."

"Well, I wasn't sure."

"I'm your brother, JD. You have annoyed me half to death since we were kids, but I always get over it. Anyway, Joseph is supposed to come home in about six months. I called because I need your help."

"All right, but first things first. Are you drinking again, Hank?"

"Occasionally," Hank said.

"Yeah. How often is occasionally?"

"Just when I need to relax."

"Just when you need to relax, huh? That kind of relaxation nearly cost me my marriage and my job. Alcoholism runs in the family, brother. Alcoholism broke Daddy's health and Mama's heart. And it was probably a drunk driver that killed Tracy."

"You have no way of knowing who killed Tracy. It was a hit and run."

"Somebody crossed double yellow on a dry road on a clear afternoon. A drunk driver is the best explanation."

"But we'll never know."

"Probably not. But in my twenty-five years as a cop, I never saw an accident of that sort that *didn't* involve alcohol. Anyway, alcohol is a temptation I struggle with daily. So do you, I imagine."

"This is why I don't call you more often, JD. I got tired of your lectures about booze a long time ago, and I don't need one tonight. I just need some help."

"All right," JD said. "What do you need?"

"I need your opinion. No, I need your honest assessment. The police... I have a gut feeling the police are not pursuing this as aggressively as they should."

"I had civilians tell me that from time to time. And in most cases, the less they understood about police work, the more impatient they were."

"If you recall, I'm not a civilian. I was a counterintelligence agent for three years, and I've done intel work for close to thirty. When there's something going on beneath the surface I can tell."

"Okay, so your gut tells you that there's something going on beneath the surface. What do you think it is?"

"I don't know yet. But here's the situation."

Hank told his brother how Ballinger had questioned him, that Jamal Wilson had refused to rat out his boss, and that Jamal Wilson had been killed. Finally, he told JD that Jamal Wilson had been shot, not stabbed like Ballinger had said.

"Shot from five hundred yards while working on a prison farm? But that detective made a point of telling you he'd been shanked." JD whistled through his teeth. "Oh yeah, this is a cover-up. You're an intelligence officer. You're trained to figure out what you can't see based on what you *can* see. Just be careful. The criminal underworld is not something civilians should dive into. And cops *really* don't like it when civilians meddle in their business."

"I know that. But I'm afraid if I don't do anything about the man who shot Sabine, I'll go nuts or drink myself to death."

"That's always a possibility with the men in our family."

"It burns me up to know that man is still free," Hank said. He switched the phone to his left ear and closed his eyes. "On the other hand, I'm afraid that if I take matters into my own hands, I'll ..."

"You'll *what?*"

"I don't know. I just know that I've had my fill of war. But I have to do *something.*"

"If you cross the line and do something criminal, protect your family from it. Don't let them know."

"I'm not going to do anything criminal," Hank said.

"You say that now, brother, but you haven't even gotten your feet wet. You got no idea what you're capable of until you start dealing with criminals on their terms."

Hank realized he was squeezing his cell phone as if it were another can of club soda. "I'm sorry to bother you with all this." He opened his eyes and relaxed his grip.

"That's what brothers are for. By the way, have you told the detective or anybody else in the department you have a brother who is a retired cop?"

"No."

"Well don't. If you want to tick off the whole department, just tell that detective that you have a brother who's a cop and then play armchair quarterback to what they're doing. Come to think of it, don't tell anybody — and I mean anybody — that you've been talking to me. I will help you any way I can, but it's best that I keep a low profile."

"You got it, JD. Listen, I'll call back in a couple of days, if you don't mind."

"Any time."

"Hey, JD?"

"Yeah?"

"Thank you."

"Any time, brother."

Hank fell back deeper into his recliner and felt the machinery of his mind speeding up despite the beer and whiskey. He lay all the way back, closed his eyes, and let the right hemisphere of his brain lead him through the gallery of images surrounding Sabine's shooting. He imagined the sound of the blue-eyed man's voice, the sensation of the beer and wine showering him in the cooler, and the sight of Sabine lying slumped over the steering wheel. He recalled Tommy muttering "Oh, Jesus," again and again.

Ten minutes later, he rose and darted upstairs to Paul's room. *This will be my workshop.* He glanced around the room at Paul's bookshelves, which held mostly books on hunting and hiking, but were topped by a row of wrestling trophies and one skeet shooting trophy. He pulled open the drawers of Paul's dresser and conducted a quick inventory. Twelve boxes ought to do. Hank made a mental diagram of where his desk should sit, where the projector table should sit, and which wall was best suited for a large map of Cumberland County.

Now that he had a general operational framework and identified the need for physical training, Hank needed an ethical framework. He searched his memories for guidance. There was Psalm 144, of course, which stated, "Praise be the Lord my Rock, who trains my hands for war, my fingers for battle." And, of course, Sun Tzu's concept of the "moral law," which certainly supported his self-appointed mission. On the other hand, Romans 13:1-4 made it clear that the powers of this world were justified, which meant that his efforts should focus on assisting the police.

I can't do this just for myself, and I can't let it be about revenge. I need to help the police, not get in their way or take the law into my own hands. What I am about to do is both moral and legal. It's just a little unorthodox.

Although Hank was not seeking a personal confrontation, he had to be prepared for a physical fight. That meant getting in shape and training for close-quarter combat, both with and without firearms. The blue-eyed man was larger and likely younger than Hank, and that meant he had to be prepared to get hurt.

Finally, Hank dropped to his knees, closed his eyes, and prayed aloud. "God, I know I ask a lot, but please bless this endeavor. Grant me the wisdom to understand, the tenacity to follow the leads, and the common sense to put it all in perspective. Please let me stay focused on justice. Don't let me fall into the pit of vengefulness. Nurture in me the skills I need to prevail in this struggle. Lead me to this man. In Jesus' name, Amen."

As Hank climbed the stairs to his and Sabine's bedroom, he thought about the early morning phone call he had received and the threatening phone call Tommy had told him about. He pulled his H&K45 out of the safe, chambered a round, and placed it on the nightstand.

"I should have shot him," he said to the ceiling. "But I didn't. Now I'll have to hunt him down."

18

Fayetteville, North Carolina
November 2, 2008

Hank pulled into the parking lot of Riverside Baptist Church and looked at his GPS watch. It was 10:40 AM. Since services started at eleven, it was too early to avoid conversations with church members if he walked in now. He leaned back and imagined answering the obvious questions. In his mind, he could hear the pastor's voice saying, "Welcome back, Hank. How was it over there? How is Sabine doing?" War and Sabine were precisely the two topics he didn't want to talk about.

The H&K45 dug into his lower right back as he gripped the wheel and pressed against the seat. The crushing sensation from the night before threatened to return, but the threats subsided after a few seconds. He listened to the radio for a few minutes and tried to pull himself together.

As he scanned radio stations, Brandon and Abby scurried past, Brandon carrying Abby's guitar case. He slumped down in his seat and sat still so they wouldn't see him. *Good God, I'm acting like some weird stalker.* Hank turned up the radio and caught part of a sermon. He listened for a few minutes as a radio preacher talked about Paul's "Mars Hill Apologetic." Hank had heard the story before. The bottom line was that Paul's speech had failed to convert the intelligentsia of Athens.

Hank turned off the radio in time to hear the chorus of the church's opening hymn, "Near the Cross." Hank knew the words from his childhood, so he hummed along with the chorus:

In the cross, in the cross
Be my glory ever
Till my raptured soul shall find
Rest beyond the river

When the hymn ended, he started the engine and drove away. He had heard a sermon and listened to a hymn. That should give him credit for attending church today. Besides, he had work to do.

Instead of going home, Hank drove by the convenience store where Sabine had been shot, passing it in the same direction and speed she had driven that night. He turned into the grocery store parking lot and eased her Escape into the same space where Sabine had parked. After checking his surroundings for a tail, he got out and retraced his steps to the convenience store.

As he rounded the corner to the front of the store, Hank noted the position of the streetlight, the traffic light at the intersection, and the distance to the wooded lot across from the store. That patch of woods was where Sabine's shooter had fled to. Obviously, he wasn't a city boy.

Hank glanced to his right as he passed the door of the convenience store. A middle-aged woman he did not recognize was working the register. He then looked at the bank parking lot across the street from the wooded lot. He pulled out his cell phone and selected the camera app as he crossed the street.

The dominant feature of the wooded lot was a short dirt pull-off that allowed access to a green metal utility box. He stepped carefully on the brush and pine needles and not on the parallel dirt tracks as he neared the utility box. As Hank expected, there were tracks around the utility box, tracks made by work boots like those Sabine's shooter had worn. No other tracks were discernible in the gray North Carolina sand. Three weeks had passed, and at least three days' rainfall. He should have checked here earlier. Still, he took a couple of photos of the tread patterns.

He put his cell phone away and walked across the street to the bank's parking lot. There he walked a clockwise circuit around the lot, noting the locations of the bank's security cameras. The back corner of the bank parking lot, under the shade of a knotty pine, was a dead zone. He strolled into the shade, turned, and looked back at the convenience store. From beneath the knotty pine, he could see the store's parking lot clearly, but could not see anything approaching the store from the rear. Someone approaching from the grocery store, as Hank had done, wouldn't be visible until they walked in front of the store. And once in front, they wouldn't be visible because an ice bin blocked the view from here. Hank snapped a few photos of the store.

The lookout car was probably parked here. That would explain a lot. There was only one car in the parking lot when Sabine and I drove past. Hank pantomimed talking on a cell phone and glanced back toward the dirt pull-off in the wooded lot. When the lookout saw the only car in the parking lot pull away, he gave the word for Jamal Wilson and the blue-eyed man to go. From this location, the lookout would not have seen Hank walk in. And if Hank hadn't been inside the beer cooler, Jamal Wilson probably would have shot him on sight. Did he owe his life to dumb luck? It wouldn't be the first time.

One other thought bothered Hank. If the overwatch element had been here, in the bank parking lot, why didn't *they* have the AR-15 to provide covering fire for the withdrawal? Having the escape vehicle provide covering fire for the withdrawal was difficult, risked fratricide.

It also left a time gap when there was no covering fire as the driver stowed the weapon and drove away.

While most analysts looked at why the enemy did certain things, Hank found it useful to look at why the enemy *didn't* do certain things. Hank knew that when a small unit didn't do what seemed sensible, it was usually due to leadership, personnel, equipment, training, or trust, so he considered each factor. The tall man was a strong leader. The group had at least four personnel. They had at least one AR-15. And the shooter was well trained. That ruled out everything except trust. And that meant that the lookouts were not trusted with an AR-15.

Samantha was working as the charge nurse that evening when Hank walked into the ICU. She looked up from her station and smiled as he walked in.

"There are only three patients here tonight," she said, "so you can stay as long as you want."

"Thank you."

Hank tiptoed into the ICU. After four weeks of visiting every night, he still felt the need to be unobtrusive. He knelt to pray and then sat beside Sabine, her hand in his.

"It's been a good day, honey," he whispered. "I had breakfast at Pete's. He says hello, and to tell you that he's praying for you. He wants us to go striper fishing with him next spring. I got an email from Paul. He's doing well, but he didn't include a lot of details, except that he qualified expert with the M249. That's a pretty big deal for an infantryman. Miss Helen mobilized the casserole brigade to make sure I stay fed, but they only come by about twice a week now. When you wake up, please don't tell Miss Helen how much I hate green bean casserole."

Hank changed his grip so that he could feel her radial pulse. He glanced back toward the nurses' station. "And I visited the store where you were shot. I'm starting to understand what happened." He sat with his eyes closed, holding her hand. *God, please wake her up.*

Abby walked in with her guitar and pulled up a chair, but Hank kept his eyes closed and said nothing. He just sat holding Sabine's hand as Abby played an instrumental version of 'Amazing Grace.' When she finished her song, she stayed. He knelt to pray again, while Abby played a few soft notes.

"I thought you had church on Sunday nights," Hank said when he returned to his chair.

"Tonight, we had a Thanksgiving service instead of our usual Sunday night service, and I preferred coming here."

"Well, it's good to see you. I really enjoyed the concert last night."

"I'm glad."

"Maybe it's my imagination, but Sabine always seems to smile when you play for her."

"When I play for her, I'm playing for you, too," Abby said.

A few minutes later, Hank walked Abby back to her car without being asked. He looked around to make sure no one was waiting in the parking lot.

"Hank," Abby said, "there's something I need to tell you. There was no Thanksgiving event at church tonight. I came here because I saw you in the church parking lot this morning, but I didn't see you in the service."

"So, now you know what an outcast I am. I don't fit in at church any better than I do in crowded bars. Was this Thanksgiving event another joke of yours that I fell for?"

"More like a cover story."

"You just blew your cover."

"Yeah, but since you won't come to church, I'll do what it takes to bring church to you."

19

Fayetteville, North Carolina
November 3, 2008

Hank awoke feeling energetic and focused. He looked at the pillow where Sabine's head should have been, and then out his bedroom window at the trees in their late autumn near-nakedness. Old oaks, proud but weather-beaten, stood guard just past the edge of his backyard fence, along with a few slender young poplars. He studied the twisted branches of the oaks and groaned. There was no way around what lay ahead. Today was just going to hurt.

After black coffee, a bottle of Muscle Milk, a half-liter of water, and an apple, he made a telephone call. Then he walked outside and opened the garage. Sunlight spilled in, revealing the gutted hulk of a red 1968 Chevy Camaro. Hank cleared the junk from around the car, a process that took the better part of an hour until he made enough room to get a tow truck close. The tow truck arrived right on schedule at nine o'clock. Hank handed the driver the title and the keys, filled out some papers, and pocketed fifty-seven hundred dollars.

An hour later, Hank loaded several boxes of car parts and assorted garage junk into his Toyota pickup. Then he drove to the county recycling center. By lunchtime, he was on his way back home from Dick's Sporting Goods with a heavy bag, a light bag, a jump rope, a chin-up and dip rack, a box of rubber matting, a pair of grip-master hand strengtheners, and a set of dumbbells. He hauled off another load of junk just before supper. After supper, he began transforming his garage into a gym. By nine in the evening, he had assembled the chin-up rack. When he was done, Hank craved a cold beer, but cracked open a can of club soda instead. He stood in the garage, admiring his work.

He put on his gloves and attacked the heavy bag with a flurry of punches and even a few Tae Kwon Do kicks. After that, he hung from the chin-up bar and did knee lifts. Tired from a busy, productive day, he took a melatonin, washed it down with a can of club soda, and prayed. Just before lying down, he placed his H&K on the nightstand. Then he fell immediately into a deep and dreamless sleep.

The next morning, Hank worked his chest and shoulders with the dumbbells as the sun rose. Then he showered and drove to Pete's for an early breakfast of steak and eggs. He skipped the hash browns. During a lull in business, Pete came over to Hank's table and the two chatted over coffee. Hank told Pete only the vaguest outlines of what he planned to do, but he knew that was all the information Pete needed.

When a crowd of six came in, Pete excused himself to serve them. Hank left so he could be at Dick's Sporting Goods when they opened the doors at nine. There, he bought a rowing machine and a treadmill and arranged to have them delivered that afternoon. On the way home, he bought fifteen boxes from the UPS Store on Ramsey Street. At home, he forced himself to pack up most of his books, even his military history books, except for two dozen that he kept out for Michael and Paul. He sold most of the books to the used bookstore near Big Jim's Gun & Pawn Shop and donated the rest to Goodwill. At Big Jim's, Hank bought 500 rounds of .45 ACP ammo for his H&K. Then he drove home, arriving just in time to take delivery of the rower and treadmill. After setting them up, he called his neighbor Willie.

"Hello?"

"Willie, this is Hank."

"Hey, Hank. Welcome home. I was hoping you would call."

Hank made the obligatory small talk, discussing this year's corn crop and whether the winter would be as hard as the last. After a few minutes, their conversation reached a natural pause.

"So, what's on your mind, Hank? You want to come by for a glass of Janelle's iced tea?"

"I do, but not today. I just wanted to let you know that I'm going to be shooting some targets in the woods behind the house, if you don't mind. When you hear gunshots down there, it's just me doing some ballistic therapy. Your dogs are not in any danger, okay?"

"That's fine, Hank. Listen, I'm real sorry about Sabine, and I'm sorry Janelle and I haven't asked you to come by already."

"That's all right, Willie, I know I've been in your and Janelle's prayers."

"You sure have, but we'd also like to have you in our living room. When can you come by?"

Hank thought for a moment. "One day next week."

As he unpacked, assembled, and arranged the exercise equipment, Hank thought about Ballinger's likely reasons for lying. None of them were good. In the end, he decided that uncovering Ballinger's reasons for lying was less important than gathering information about the man who shot Sabine. Besides, Ballinger's reasons just might surface along the way.

When he was done, Hank took a deep breath and dialed Ballinger's office number.

"Ballinger."

"Yeah, this is Hank McCaskill. I was hoping you could give me an update on the man who shot my wife."

"There's no new developments, Major, or I would have called. We're still hoping something will come out of the investigation into the murder of Jamal Wilson. But we have to wait for Caledonia prison to tell us what they've got. So far, they haven't told us much."

"What do we do next, now that Jamal Wilson is dead?" he asked Detective Ballinger.

"There's not a lot I can do. I got no face, no fingerprints, and no name, so I can't search through databases."

"Detective Ballinger, you just told me the things we *can't* do. Tell me what we *can* do."

"What *you* can do is be patient. What *I* can do is check the adjacent counties, look for robberies with a similar modus operandi and similar perps, that sort of thing. It's a long shot, but sometimes we get lucky and find a connection to similar crimes."

"Makes sense. What do you think he will do next?"

"I expect he'll lay low because he thinks someone got killed," Ballinger answered. "Whoever he is, I don't think he's stupid."

"How about this?" Hank said. "He lies low for a little while. Then, when he needs money again, he robs again. He starts with a thorough reconnaissance. Identifies the alarm buttons, locations of the cash bags, and the name of the cashier. After that, he disables the security camera. Along the way, he finds a new accomplice."

"Sure. I could buy that. But where, and when?"

"Well, without any structured analysis to go on, it's hard to say, but once I begin analyzing crime data, I may be able to predict his next move."

"Analyzing crime data?"

"Yes. Predictive analysis starts with good data."

"Predictive analysis? Who do you think you are, Nosferatu?"

"I think you mean Nostradamus," Hank replied. "Nosferatu was a vampire in a horror movie. Nostradamus was a French mystic. Sixteenth century, I believe, and quite a con artist, if you ask me."

"Whatever. My point is that you can't predict crime."

"Actually, you can. Or rather, *we* can if I have the resources to dig into it. There's an entire field of study called Criminal Intelligence."

"Look, Major, I've been a cop for twelve years. I know what Criminal Intelligence is. There's this girl here at headquarters who uses CompStat to churn out statistics for the chief. It's all hocus-pocus if you ask me."

"You're talking about operational statistics. I'm talking about tactical criminal intelligence. Those are two different disciplines. If you just let me help you by doing some tactical intelligence, I may be able to predict where this guy will strike next. You make the arrest and get the glory. All I want is for him to be taken down."

"Right. Listen, Major, I have a fresh homicide case I'm working this month, so I have to go, but I'll contact you immediately if there's any new developments in your wife's case."

Hank's voice hardened. "And the Jamal Wilson case?"

"Yeah. That one too."

"Thank you for your time, Detective Ballinger," Hank said, certain that Ballinger had not detected his sarcasm.

"Sure thing."

That afternoon, as Fox News droned in the background, Hank disassembled his H&K45 as if it were precious jewelry. He cleaned and lubricated each moving part and then looked through the barrel to check for grit in the grooves. He performed a functions check, worked the slide a few times, and practiced aiming by sighting in on various objects around the kitchen. After that, he practiced locking the slide one-handed by pressing the pistol against his thigh and pushing it forward. He practiced releasing the slide and aiming one-handed, first with his right and then with his left. After that, he practiced changing magazines, slowly at first, and then quickly as his muscle memory improved.

He took a break to drink a club soda and then practiced working the slide and changing magazines — right-handed and left-handed — with his eyes closed. Finally, he put a plastic dummy round in the chamber and turned on the television. He walked around the living room, keeping the television screen in his peripheral vision. Every time the scene changed, he drew, sighted in on the person on the screen, and squeezed the trigger. He then practiced drawing and firing from various other positions: standing, kneeling, squatting, and even flat on this back, the barrel of his H&K45 pointed just over his toes at the flickering images.

Hank holstered his pistol and grabbed several boxes of ammunition. He walked out to the back yard, where he witnessed a glorious orange sunset and inhaled the aroma of falling leaves and moist earth. Hank vaulted over the fence and walked to the gully, where he fired ten rounds into the embankment to regain a feel for the pistol's recoil. Then he set up a silhouette target about fifteen meters away and began firing more deliberately. After firing the first hundred rounds, he switched hands and fired left-handed. Then he practiced drawing and firing in one motion. After that, Hank fired fifty rounds from various nonstandard positions: kneeling, prone, seated, and on his back.

So much for basic drills and self-directed practice. I'll soon need professional instruction. I'll also need more ammo. He looked at the fading sunlight and felt an autumn chill setting in as he headed home. When he hopped back over the fence, he glanced at his tomato patch, which lay wilted, weed-choked, and half-forgotten. He needed to tend to the tomato patch this week or next week.

Once inside, Hank popped the top on a club soda, sat in his recliner, and downed a few gulps. After that, he ate a dinner of boneless, skinless chicken breasts and garbanzo beans as he thought about the coming winter. While he ate, he imagined Sabine lying unconscious in a hospital bed, circled by Christmas decorations. *No.* He closed his eyes and imagined her at home, lying back on his recliner, a blanket draped over her legs, weak, but smiling.

After dinner, he put the H&K in the refrigerator for twenty minutes and then practiced working the action. The cold metal hurt his hands, but he welcomed the pain. Then he wet his hands under the kitchen sink and practiced working his cold gun until his fingers went numb. After that, he cleaned and lubricated the H&K yet again.

After changing into shorts and a tee shirt, Hank spent half an hour online, browsing through ballistic vests. *Based on what happened to Jamal Wilson, I need something that will stop large-caliber jacketed rounds.* After checking the specs on several models, he selected a level IIIA vest, which was advertised as being "engineered to achieve the #1 comfort rating by customer reviews," and would protect against most pistol-caliber rounds. He also clicked the box to include the accompanying level IV insert plate, which the specs claimed would stop rifle rounds up to 30-06. Satisfied with his selections, he looked at the computer and said, "My frugal Schwabian *hausfrau* approves this purchase." Then he clicked the order button.

Next, Hank did a Google search on "criminal intelligence analysis." Based on the results, he ordered three books: *Criminal Intelligence Analysis using Microsoft Office, Crime Analysis in 60 Steps,* and *Fundamentals of Intelligence-Led Policing.* After that, he researched hardware requirements for ArcGIS mapping software. Once he had identified the hardware requirements, he checked to see the laptop computers in stock at the Fort Bragg PX. He selected one that would meet those requirements. Then he bought a projector from Amazon that would be compatible with the laptop.

Next, Hank searched the telephone book and identified four print shops in the Fayetteville area. At least one of them should be able to print a five-foot-by-five-foot map. He sent Pete an email and chased a melatonin capsule with a can of club soda.

When he was almost ready for bed, Hank stood in front of the bathroom mirror, brushing his teeth. "I'm not going to take the law into my own hands, Sabine," he muttered around his toothbrush. "I'm just going to give the police a little help."

20

Iqbal and three other young men stood in the kitchen of the old farm-house, illuminated only by the yellow light from a kerosene lantern. The blue-eyed man flipped a light switch, but no lights came on. Then he pushed open a rotting wooden door. The aromas of mold and sweat rose as he led them down a creaky staircase into a concrete-block basement that extended the length of the farmhouse. Large, exposed beams crossed the basement's ceiling. One beam held a grimy heavy bag aloft. Beyond that, a stack of padded mats lay on the concrete.

"I bought a generator last week," he said as he turned around, "but the basement is the only room I wired. I need to introduce y'all to some basic hand-to-hand combat moves. If Jamal had been better trained, he could have parried the blow that knocked him out."

"All right. That sounds, um, *prudent*," Amal said. The young men looked around at the basement while the blue-eyed man changed into a muscle shirt. He strutted to the heavy bag and glared at it while he stretched.

Moments later, he threw a few half-speed jabs and then bounced on his toes and swayed his body back and forth. He let loose with a series of punches: a strong jab, another jab followed by a cross, and then a rapid jab-cross-hook, and finally, a powerful jab-cross-hook. He hit the bag harder and faster until he worked himself into a frenzy. Then he lashed out with a muay thai push kick that hit the bag at the level of a man's groin. He followed that with another powerful right hook. As the bag rocked back, he dodged, ducked, and then laid into it with a tae kwon do roundhouse kick. The pop of the kick's impact caused Amal and Iqbal to jump and even seemed to shake the beams of the house.

He turned to the boys, grinning through the sheen of sweat on his face. "Amal, what does the Koran say about those killed in the path of God?"

Amal smiled. "Do not say of those who are killed in the path of God, 'They are dead.' They are alive."

"Correct," the man said. He threw a flurry of punches into the middle of the bag. "Bilal," he said, "what did Sayyid Qutb say is the reason human beings suffer?"

Iqbal leaned toward Bilal and started to whisper, but the blue-eyed man shook his head, causing Iqbal to straighten up and remain silent.

"Because they are imperfect?" Bilal answered.

"Wrong answer!" The man spun and launched a side-thrust kick that nearly knocked the bag loose from its anchor in the crossbeam. Bilal jumped back as the man continued. "They suffer because they violate the laws of Allah. You need to spend less time playing video games and more time studying the Koran and going to the gym."

"Daood, which sura of the Koran addresses the spoils of war?"

Daood looked at the floor in silence. The man punched the bag a few times while scowling at Daood. "Al Anfal, Daood, *Al Anfal.* That's pretty basic."

His gaze fell upon Iqbal. "Iqbal, what did Sayyid Qutb say was the ideal society?"

"One ruled by the sovereignty of Allah as expressed in Sharia law."

"Excellent, Iqbal. Excellent."

Iqbal smiled and stood a little taller.

"Now, pay attention, all of you," the blue-eyed man said. "If you study and train hard, in a few weeks, you'll be able to throw punches and kicks like this."

"Yes, I will," Amal said, flashing a grin. Daood, Bilal, and Iqbal remained silent, but Iqbal stared in wide-eyed wonder as Amal stepped forward and punched the bag.

"I am ready to learn these punches and kicks," Amal said.

Iqbal studied the heavy bag as it rocked and swayed on its chain under Amal's clumsy but enthusiastic assault.

21

After a short jog and a light breakfast, Hank entered his garage, his eyes fixed on the two men in front of him. He snapped into a fighting stance and raised his hands in front of him. He moved his hands forward into a fighting position and clenched his bare feet to grip the gymnastics mat. One of his opponents was a tall, thin man with blue eyes, the other stocky, and dark-haired: Lieutenant Upton and Sergeant Chapman. A third man, Specialist Davis, stood in the corner, dressed in shorts and a tee shirt, his arms crossed.

Hank and his two opponents wore boxing helmets, groin protectors, and footpads. They squeezed their hands into fingerless martial arts gloves and so did Hank. Although neither opponent was armed, Hank knew that the coming fight probably would not end in his favor. He circled cautiously, waiting for the two men to make the first move so he would know which opponent was more aggressive.

Chapman lunged at Hank as if he were going to try a tackle, but then drew back and threw a few inconclusive jabs. Hank was not a skilled boxer, but he had a little bit of training, so he swatted the jabs away and threw a right cross. Chapman dodged the right and tagged Hank with a glancing right cross of his own. Although the blow was ineffective, it distracted Hank for an instant, which enabled Upton to strike with a rear kick that seemed to come out of nowhere. Hank blocked the kick, but the inertia knocked him a few feet sideways and right into the path of another right cross by Chapman. Hank ducked a second punch, spun, and hit Chapman with a quick side-thrust kick that knocked him down.

At just that moment, a barrel-chested young man with a precise flat top walked into the garage. He looked around at the weights and exercise equipment that had been moved aside.

"Michael!" Hank shouted. "Glad you're here. I could use some help."

"Dad, you're retired. What are you thinking?"

"We're training," Hank answered. "You should join us."

The instant Hank took his eyes off his opponents, Chapman caught him in the abdomen with a front-snap kick. Hank grunted and doubled over. Before he could stand upright, Upton tackled him and drove him into the mat.

"Pay attention, sir," Davis said. "Never take your eyes off your opponent!"

"Hey, you must be Major McCaskill's son," Chapman said as Hank and Upton rolled around the mat like high school wrestlers.

Michael nodded.

"I'm Aaron. Nice to meet you," Chapman said, taking off his right glove to shake Michael's hand. "That's Davis in the corner," he said with a nod of his head. "He can't talk now because he's coaching your dad."

Michael shook Chapman's hand, but his eyes never left the mat where Upton was tying his father into a virtual pretzel. Michael looked surprised when Hank hooked a leg around Upton's abdomen and turned him on his back in a quick reverse.

"Your old man's pretty quick," Chapman said.

"Way to break it, sir!" Davis yelled. "Now get on top!"

Hank wound up on his side, his legs around Upton's midsection. Upton waved at Michael from a prone position. "Hey. I'm Lieutenant Upton," he said, and then his voice degenerated into a grunt as Hank squeezed the air out of him.

"Excuse me, Michael," Chapman said. He shoved his hand back into his glove and darted into the fray. Chapman punched Hank in the head, almost knocking Upton loose from Hank's leg-lock. When the first punch failed to free Upton, Chapman pulled his leg back to kick Hank, but Hank grabbed Chapman's leg, blocking the kick.

Chapman landed a quick left jab as Hank pulled him to the mat. All three men were now writhing on the mat.

Davis looked on and shook his head. "Very sloppy. That's it for now. Take a break."

"Come on, Davis, I pretty well had him," Hank protested.

"No, you didn't," Upton said.

Hank glared at Upton, who added, "sir."

"Okay, fine. Let's take a break," Hank said. He and Upton stood up and bumped gloves.

"Good fight, sir," Upton said.

"Thanks. Good fight, Lieutenant," Hank replied.

"Hey, Lieutenant, let's go get something to drink," Chapman said.

"Sounds good," Upton replied. The two men went into the house.

"Davis, you're probably thirsty too," Chapman yelled. "Get in here."

"Yes, Sergeant," Davis said before following the other two men into the house.

Michael followed the men with his eyes. "Dad, who *are* these guys?"

"They told you their names, son. The stocky guy with the Texas accent is Aaron Chapman, and the tall one is Charles Upton. The guy with shoulders like an NBA player is Jay Davis. They're soldiers who worked for me in Iraq. Davis is a qualified Level III combatives instructor and a Mixed Martial Arts fighter. He knows his stuff."

"So, why is a retired guy holding MMA fights in the garage?"

"They're helping me train."

"Helping you train? It looks more like they're beating the snot out of you."

"Yep, that's probably what it looks like."

"Dad, your nose is bleeding," Michael said.

"Better to shed a little blood in training than a lot of blood in war," Hank said.

"Didn't you say you were done with war?"

"You know, I have some old workout clothes you could wear. You should join us."

"Thanks, but I get plenty of combatives training at Camp Lejeune. And don't think I didn't notice how you didn't answer my question."

"You caught that, huh? Well, I *am* done with war, but I'm not done seeking justice."

"Dad, your eye is starting to swell up."

"Could you fetch me the bag of frozen peas from the door of the freezer? I know my eye is going to be black, but I don't want it to be swollen shut. I need to see well enough to shoot some targets tomorrow morning."

"Shoot some targets, huh?"

"Are you coming up for Thanksgiving?" Hank asked. "Paul's going to be here."

Michael shook his head. "Madison and I are going to spend Thanksgiving with her family in Charleston."

Just then, Chapman called out from the kitchen, "Hey Michael, your old man is a pretty good fighter."

"You think so?"

"Yeah, for a man his age, I mean."

Afternoon sunlight streamed through the brown-leafed oak branches, bright but cold. Hank stood loosely; his right hand poised over his holstered H&K. He shifted his weight and looked over his shoulder at Pete, who stood behind him. Pete held Sabine's mechanical egg timer in one hand and a stopwatch in the other.

Hank nodded and turned to face the two football dummies that faced him. One was less than an arm's length in front of him. The other was about nine feet away. Both had paper silhouettes stapled to them. Pete had nicknamed the dummies "Bill One" and "Bill Two," but Hank didn't know why. Hank had insisted on stapling ski masks on both.

"Get ready," Pete said.

Hank dropped into a crouch and felt a rage boiling up inside him. Just as he gritted his teeth in anger, the egg timer went off. Startled, he stiff-armed Bill One so hard that the dummy fell to the ground. Hank fired three rounds, two of which grazed the dummy. Then he whirled to his right and fired three times in rapid succession. Only one round struck Bill Two.

Hank held the pistol out so that Pete could see that it was empty and safe.

"Settle down, Hank. Don't be angry. You got like this back in Arauca—"

"I remember." Hank said.

"You nearly shot your own left hand because you held the stiff-arm too long. At point-blank range, it's gonna be quick and deadly. No second chances. You got to relax and force yourself to go slow and smooth. Slow gets you smooth, smooth gets you fast. Now take a deep breath and relax. Then, when I say 'now,' the timer will be set for anywhere from fifteen seconds to three minutes. Don't draw before the timer goes off."

Hank exhaled and stretched his arms. "Let's do it again."

"Get ready."

Hank waited in a crouched position until his lower back began to ache. He concentrated on controlling his breathing and entering the state of wary detachment that he would need to survive a gunfight. As the first twenty seconds crawled by, Hank felt himself entering the zone. The wind tugged at the silhouette stapled to Bill One. A pair of squirrels darted around the oak trees overhead, and a dog barked in the distance. He took in the smells of the forest in autumn and felt something stirring deep inside his mind when the egg timer buzzed.

Hank stiff-armed Bill One and stepped back as he drew his H&K. He hip-fired two rounds into the dummy's midsection, extended his arm, and fired a third round into its head. Then Hank spun to his right, took the pistol with both hands, and fired two rounds into Bill Two's midsection. He fired a third into Bill Two's head.

"Clear?" Pete asked.

Hank held his pistol so Pete could see that the pistol was clear. He straightened and turned to look at Pete.

"Not bad that time," Pete said. "Less than four seconds, and your time will come down as we practice. But look at your first two shots on Bill Two. They're low and left. You're bulldogging that trigger. It's not really a factor at this distance, but at five yards and seven yards, you might miss your first two shots. That could give Bill Two enough time to kill you."

Over the next twenty minutes, Hank and Pete repeated this drill until Hank developed the muscle memory to stiff-arm Bill One and put three rounds into him and then shoot Bill Two in just under three seconds. Then they walked back until Bill One was at three yards and Bill Two was at five and repeated the drill without the stiff-arm. When Hank's times were well within three seconds, they walked both dummies out to seven yards.

"You're anticipating the recoil and overworking the trigger. Let's do some recoil drills and trigger control drills before you shoot the sevens," Pete said. He took the pistol from Hank and tucked it under his arm. Pete grinned and held up one bullet and one blue dummy round. Hank closed his eyes until he heard Pete slide a magazine into the pistol and chamber a round. Pete handed it back to Hank and grinned.

"I think I know what's next," Hank said.

"You got a fifty-fifty chance. This shot could be a snap cap, or it could be a live round. Let's see just how badly you're anticipating the recoil. Fire when ready."

Hank crouched again and squeezed the trigger. *Click.* The firing pin struck a dummy round instead of a live round, but Hank flinched and pushed the pistol down and to the left.

"See what I mean?" Pete said. "We're going to do this about fifty times until you hold that pistol rock steady for a dummy round. And try not to squeeze the grip so hard with your pinky. That's another thing that's pulling your point of impact down and left."

For the next twenty minutes, Hank worked to reduce his anticipation of the pistol's recoil. After that, Pete had him balance an empty casing on the top of the pistol's slide. He dry-fired it until he could squeeze the trigger without making the casing fall off.

At long last, they repeated the egg-timer draw and shoot drill against Bill One and Bill Two at seven yards. Hank consistently six out of six within three seconds.

"You shoot pretty well," Pete said, "but you're not quite at the level you need to be. If you're right about this guy, you need to be at the top of your game when things go south. And things always go south."

"I remember," Hank said.

22

Fayetteville, North Carolina
Friday, November 28, 2008

The day after Thanksgiving, Hank awoke early and lifted weights with Paul. Then Paul left to go hunting on Willie's land. Hank was almost halfway through normalizing the mountains of data he had downloaded when the doorbell rang. He sprang down the stairs and was surprised to find Abby standing on the porch.

"I know I'm a little early," she said, "but my roommate is out of town, and I'm caught up on studying."

"Early for what?" Hank asked.

"I thought Paul would have told you I was coming by."

"He didn't," Hank said, but he let Abby inside. As she stepped into the foyer, she looked at the family photographs adorning the walls. She smiled at Hank and Sabine's wedding photo.

"I've always liked that photo. Sabine looks beautiful in it."

"I've always thought so," Hank said. "Now, I need to—"

"Is that your brother in the police uniform?"

"Yes. My brother JD was a cop in Atlanta. Anyway, I'm going to head upstairs to my workshop—"

"I've always thought your sons looked cute in those little soldier outfits," Abby said, giggling as she looked at another photo. "By the way, where is Michael today? Paul said I might get to see him."

"Um, Michael is spending Thanksgiving with Madison and her family down in Charleston. Paul went hunting early this morning."

"Who went with him?"

"Nobody. He got up early and snuck outside without a sound. With a little luck, we'll be making a trip to the deer processor this afternoon."

"That would be good for us," Abby said, "but not so good for the deer." Her gaze wandered about the dusty living room, her eyes widening when she noticed the entertainment center. "Oh, you still have your vinyl records!" she said. "And your old turntable!"

"Junk I never bothered to get rid of."

"Why would you get rid of them?"

Hank glanced at his watch. "One, they're in the way, and two, they take up a lot more space than CDs, and three, I have a lot of them on iTunes now."

"Does your turntable still work?"

"I suppose it does, but I haven't used it much since 9-11. And the sound quality of analog is just not that—"

"The sound quality of analog is fine," Abby said.

Hank looked at his watch, sighed, and forced a smile. "Anyway, I bought one of those turntables that makes digital audio files from vinyl. I started with the A's and only made it through ABBA before 9-11 happened. Just to be clear, the old ABBA records are *Sabine's*, not mine. Anyway, my plan was to make digital copies of my record collection and then sell the vinyl. Make some money and save space. Then, after 9-11, my life got pretty busy. That was more than seven years ago. I never got to B."

"I'm glad you didn't sell them," Abby said. She pulled the LP *Infinity* by Journey out of the stack.

"You recognize that?" Hank asked, laughing.

"Yeah! This one has *'Wheel in the Sky'*!"

"Yes, it does. But what's the story behind your fascination with vinyl?"

She took the sleeve out of the cover with an air of reverence and laid it on the turntable.

"For one thing, vinyl records make me nostalgic. Aunt Melissa inherited a huge collection of vinyl records from my grandparents. She was born in December 1972, and my grandparents named her after the song by the Allman Brothers."

At last, she placed the LP on the turntable, and she and Hank listened to *"Wheel in the Sky"* in reverent silence. As the last notes faded, Hank spoke.

"So, you're a twenty-year-old who's fascinated with vinyl."

"My friends tell me I'm an old soul. Anyway, listening to a vinyl album requires *commitment*. It's not like a CD or a digital file. You have to use two hands to take a record out of the sleeve. The artwork on an album is also large, so you have to work it loose from the sleeve. Vinyl albums are unified pieces of art: the cover, the liner notes, everything. When you were a kid, did you ever sit on the floor, close your eyes, and just listen — I mean really listen — to a vinyl record? Did you ever think that technology has reduced music to background noise?"

"Aren't you too young to have thoughts like that?"

Abby's hands drew near the album with *"Forever Autumn"* by Justin Hayward, and Hank remembered the song's effect on him from her performance at the Steam Room. He stood abruptly. "I need to finish what I was doing in my workshop."

"Please? Just one more song?" she asked.

Hank sat down again.

"You have Jeff Wayne's *'War of the Worlds'*!" she said. "These are hard to find."

"If I remember correctly, I found it at a yard sale in the eighties for about two dollars. I have other records you may like better."

"I don't think so. This is a real pearl."

"A pearl, huh? You know, a pearl starts out as a painful irritant to some unlucky oyster. Over time, the oyster turns the irritant into something beautiful. Then, just when the oyster has made something beautiful, he gets hauled ashore, iced, shucked, and eaten. Game over."

"Aren't you just a sunbeam of positive energy?" Abby said. She opened the album to reveal the artwork inside and then sat to admire it. "My favorite track on this album is 'Forever Autumn.' Do you mind if I play it?"

"No, I don't mind if you play it," Hank said. After all, it was her singing, not the song itself, that made the lyrics so heartbreaking.

"I played this one a few weeks ago at the coffee shop. Do you remember?"

"I think so."

Abby took the record from the sleeve, wiped it with a dusting cloth, and placed it on the turntable. When it spun to life, the synthe-sized flutes sang like a pair of birds, sometimes in harmony and some-times singing slightly different melodies. Then she sang the first few lines in perfect time and pitch with Justin Hayward.

"Why do you have to play that one?" he asked after the first verse, his voice wavering just a little on the word "play."

"I told you. It's my favorite. You said you remembered when I played it at the coffee house."

"I said, I *think* I remember."

As Abby sang along with the second verse, Hank felt the familiar clutch of unspeakable grief squeezing his chest. His eyes burned, but he stopped himself short of crying. He stood abruptly and brushed his hands on his pants as if knocking off old dust.

"Enjoy my old music. I need to get some work done." He stood and walked toward the stairs.

At the next pause in the vocals, she said, "If you're waiting for me to apologize for playing this song, you're going to be waiting for a very long time. I'm not sorry. This song is exactly what you needed to hear. It's natural to grieve."

"You said you came here to see Paul. Seems to me you came here to annoy me. Now, I'd like to load up and analyze the rest of my eastern North Carolina crime data today."

Abby didn't say anything, she just sang the third verse and looked up at Hank expectantly. When the last vocals faded, she said, "Go play with data if that's what you think you need. Or you could sit back down and listen to some old songs."

"Those songs are history."

"So is your crime data. Besides, old souls like us enjoy history," she said.

"But when the study of history has no bearing on the present, it's just an exercise in *antiquarianism*."

"Wow. That's a big word," Abby said. "But these songs are not antiquarian." She gestured at Hank's record collection. "These songs are the soundtrack of your life."

She sang the verse about a man kicking his way alone through autumn leaves, and Hank realized that he was not safe from her voice, even though the music had stopped. He walked upstairs.

"It's only natural to grieve," she said to Hank's back.

Maybe Michael was right about her: clingy and annoying.

Ten minutes later, as Hank was downloading a batch of crime data, soft footfalls on the stairs broke his concentration. He turned from his laptop to see Abby peering through the doorway, one arm on the doorframe and half her body still in the hallway.

"You've totally redone Paul's room," Abby said. Then she stepped inside.

"Yeah. It's my workshop now. Paul said he didn't mind."

"What are you working on?"

"Not music," Hank replied. "Help yourself to my record collection. It's downstairs."

Abby looked at the computer screen and nodded. "You're trying to find the man who shot Sabine, aren't you?"

Hank locked the screen of his new laptop and swiveled his chair around to face her. "I'm building a macro-level understanding of crime patterns in the area, and then I'll work a few leads. So yes, I'm trying to find the man who shot Sabine."

Abby smiled and stepped into the room. "You want some help?"

"Yes. I want Michael and Paul to help me. And Pete, of course."

"But they're not here."

"Look, I appreciate it, but I don't want you involved in what I'm doing."

"So, you want help, just not from me."

"Have you made it your personal mission to annoy me today, young lady? Because that's what you're doing."

Abby bit her lip and looked down. "I've been friends with Paul since we were in sixth grade. Joseph and I are friends, and as for Michael, we get along for the most part. They're like the brothers I never had. And Sabine was the reason I kept going to church, even when I was thirteen and got kind of disillusioned with the whole religion thing. I always looked up to you for being a good father, but aside from my singing, you barely noticed me. I guess I'd just like to do something besides provide entertainment, okay?"

Hank nodded as twin pangs of guilt and sadness pricked his chest. "All right." He unlocked the screen and unfolded a camping chair from the corner before motioning for her to sit down.

Hank then showed her the data that he had downloaded and started to analyze, explaining how to correlate the basic characteristics of each criminal incident. She grasped the significance of each analytical parameter more quickly than Hank had expected.

"What do you think?" he asked when he was finished.

"You've got a lot of good data about the characteristics of each incident, and you know how to analyze it, but what about the people involved?"

Hank thought for a moment. "What do you mean by that?"

"I mean, you've got names, yeah, but do you really know much about them? My Uncle Sean used to tell me that when he did interviews, he was never a 'just the facts' kind of guy. He wanted to get to know the perpetrators, the witnesses, and the victims as *people*."

Hank sat upright in his chair. "And I suppose you have the time and resources to go interview everyone involved with every incident of interest in my database?"

"I don't have time, but Anne Murray does."

"Okay, I'll play your game. Who's Anne Murray, besides a Canadian singer?"

"She's my alter ego. I have two Facebook accounts. One is under my real name and the other is under the name 'Anne Murray.'"

"Facebook, huh? That's the thing that older people use as an alternative to MySpace?"

"Yeah, but it's really growing in popularity right now. I use it to check out people I meet through my band and through school and such. Uncle Sean taught me to be careful, so before I talk to someone about doing a gig, or before I go out with a guy, I log onto Facebook as Anne Murray and check them out. I read about their friends and interests, then I look at their photos. You know, just to make sure they're not creeps or crazies."

"So, you're saying I should use Facebook to collect information and build personality files on all the people involved in incidents in my database?"

"Nope," Abby said with a mischievous grin. "I'm saying you should let me do that for you. Or rather, we should let Anne Murray do it. And not all of the people, just the ones of greatest interest."

"I see," Hank said.

"If nothing else, it would save you a lot of time."

Hank rolled his chair back from his computer and motioned for Abby to pull the camping stool closer. "Let's see what you can do, starting with the name Jamal Wilson. I'm wondering if any of his previous criminal associates would have wanted him dead."

An hour later, when Hank and Abby went downstairs, Paul still hadn't returned from hunting, but Hank understood Jamal Wilson a little better. His family life was a mess, his music glorified violence, his friends goaded him into crime, and his education had ended in tenth grade. *A man of clay.* And even though Jamal Wilson had tried to kill him, Hank felt a small degree of sympathy toward the man.

"Maybe we could listen to more records until Paul gets home," Hank said.

"On one condition," Abby said. "You heard *me* sing. Now can I hear *you* sing?"

"I traded my guitar for a rifle thirty years ago, and I traded my rifle for a laptop a few years after that. I'm a soldier and an intelligence analyst, not a singer."

"You *were* a soldier."

"I'll always be a soldier. If you cut me, I'd bleed green."

"Please? Sing just one song? For me?"

Hank sat down and wondered when Paul would be back.

"I'll bet you could do justice to a Merle Haggard song," Abby said.

"I don't think so," Hank said. "It's been a few years, but I think I remember the words to 'Galveston' by Jimmy Webb."

"I've heard Glen Campbell sing 'Galveston' but I've never heard of Jimmy Webb. Did Jimmy Webb do a cover of it?"

"Oh no," Hank laughed. "Jimmy Webb wrote and recorded the *original* 'Galveston,' but Glen Campbell recorded the most famous version of it. Glen Campbell sings it too fast if you ask me, but it's still a great song."

"Let's find it," Abby said.

They started opening boxes. After a few minutes of digging, Abby found the old LP with Glen Campbell's version of 'Galveston.' She put it on the turntable and sat back down on the floor while Hank stood to sing. His voice was weak as he sang the first lines, but it gained strength as the song progressed.

"I told you Glen sings it too fast," he said after the first verse.

Abby turned the stereo up louder. When the song ended, Abby stood up and clapped.

"Why do you like this song so much?"

"It tells the story of a soldier in the Spanish-American war. He sailed from Galveston and left his girl behind and she's all he thinks about. Some people take it as an anti-war song, but to me it's just a song about the personal effects of war."

"I can see that," she agreed with a solemn nod. "So, what's your favorite part of the song?"

"The line where the narrator says he's afraid of dying before he can dry the tears she's crying."

"Why?"

The first notes of *"Take My Hand for a While"* forced Hank to speak louder. "Because a good songwriter would have stopped after describing the soldier's fear, but Jimmy Webb goes into *why* the soldier is afraid. He's not afraid of *death*, he's afraid of *dying*. Specifically, he's afraid of dying before he can fulfill his responsibilities. And that is what makes Jimmy Webb a great songwriter."

Abby said nothing, but she seemed on the verge of tears.

"What's wrong?" Hank asked.

Abby looked down and put her face in her hands. On impulse, Hank put a hand on her shoulder.

"What's wrong?" Hank asked again, more softly. Abby said nothing but stepped closer to Hank and looked up at him. She seemed about to say something when Michael stepped into the room. Upon seeing them, he stopped and crossed his arms over his muscular chest.

"Excuse me, but am I interrupting?" Michael asked with just a hint of acid in his voice. Stepping back suddenly, Hank almost fell over a box of records. Abby hid her face in her hands.

"Son, I didn't hear you come in."

"Your music was a bit loud."

"I used to tell you the same thing," Hank said as he turned the volume down.

"I remember," Michael said. He didn't smile back.

"Is everything all right, son? I thought you were spending the day with Madison."

"She and her mom wanted to go shopping. Even a Marine knows not to go up against the Black Friday crowds, so I came up here. Is Paul around?"

"He went hunting. You want something to drink?"

"Some coffee would be good. I drove all the way from Charleston with only one stop."

"Okay. I'll go make some. Abby, you want some?"

"Sure."

Abby stood and held her hand out. "Nice to see you again, Michael."

"Nice to see you, too," Michael said through clenched teeth. "I almost didn't recognize you. You're a lot thinner than you were the last time I saw you." He shook her hand but said nothing further. While Abby played *"If You Could Read My Mind,"* by Gordon Lightfoot, he followed Hank into the kitchen.

"What is she doing here?"

"She's here to see Paul. Did you know she's a professional musician now? She plays guitar and sings for wounded soldiers over at Fort Bragg, and for families of patients at the county hospital. That's where I ran into her. Therapy through music, that's her thing."

"This house is not a hospital."

"No," Hank said, "it's more like a museum these days." He made a sweeping gesture that encompassed the living room and then continued in a voice like a carnival hawker. "Welcome back, my friend to the Hank McCaskill Museum of Personal Failure. On the first floor, we have old photographs of less than perfect relationships. On the second floor, we have beds that no one sleeps in anymore. Outside, we have a backyard featuring dead tomato plants and shattered dreams."

"All right, Dad. You still speak sarcasm pretty well, but you didn't answer my question. What is she doing here alone with you?"

"She came over here to meet Paul, but he's still out hunting. In the meantime, she was helping me sort through some stuff. When you came in, we were just taking a break to listen to some old music."

"She still seems very fond of you."

"Yeah, I think so."

Michael shook his head. "Look, Dad, Miss Helen from Mom's church called me and told me you'd been spending a lot of time with Abby. I didn't believe it until now."

"So, Miss Helen has been watching the house. Is that the real reason you drove up here?"

"Dad, I don't know how to say this, but Mom is in a coma, and you've got a house guest who happens to be a younger woman. That just doesn't look good."

"You're wrong on two counts. She's not *my* house guest, she's Paul's. And it looks fine, as far as I'm concerned."

"Fine? She's the same age as Paul. That girl is young enough to be your daughter. That's just creepy."

"Creepy, huh? Maybe the age difference is the point. Maybe she sees me as a father figure. And maybe there's a hole in my heart because Sabine and I never had a daughter. And for the tenth time, she didn't come here to see *me*," Hank said. "Besides, *that girl* is one of the few friends I have since your mom got shot. People *avoid* me these days, Michael. I mean, they send cards, and they tell me they're praying for Sabine, but practically nobody calls, and nobody at all comes by. Well, nobody but Miss Helen, and she just cleans while I'm away, drops off an occasional casserole, and watches me like the KGB watching a dissident."

Michael nodded. "Okay, Dad, so you're lonely. I get it. But Abby shouldn't be here to cheer you up every time I visit."

"Then maybe you should stay away. That's something you and your brothers are pretty good at."

"Fair enough," Michael said with a downward glance. "We could be doing better."

"Look, son," Hank said, his tone softer. "I know you shouldered a lot of responsibility growing up because you are the oldest son and I was gone—"

Michael turned and walked away before Hank could finish. Hank's heart sank, and a different kind of grief gnawed at him.

Michael walked into the living room, where Abby sat cross-legged on the floor, listening to the last fading notes of "If You Could Read My Mind."

"Abby," Michael said with an artificial grin, "I have something I'd like to ask you."

"Go ahead."

"You're thirty years younger than my father," Michael began.

"Yes," Abby said, the smile fading from her face.

"And right now, while you're at his house, his wife — *my mother* — is comatose in a hospital bed. How do you think that looks?"

Abby tossed her head and pushed her hair behind her shoulder. She stood and faced Michael. "I don't *care* how it looks."

"Well, you *should*," Michael said.

Abby bit her lower lip. "Right now, the man who shot your mother is still on the loose, and you haven't done anything to help your father find him. How do you think *that* looks?"

"It looks like I have enough sense not to stick my nose into police business."

"Well, the police aren't following this as aggressively as they should."

"How could you know that?" Michael snapped. "Do you go to the police station every day for an update on the case?"

"No, but they still haven't made an arrest."

"There you go," Michael said with a roll of his eyes. "If they haven't made an arrest by now, *obviously* the police are not — what did you say? — they're not following this as aggressively as they should. By the way, when you say that, you sound like my dad."

"I'm glad one of us does," Abby said.

Just then, Hank walked into the room, balancing three cups of coffee. He handed one cup to Abby and one to Michael. Michael smiled, but there was no joy in his eyes. Hank pretended not to notice.

"Thanks," Michael said, glaring at Hank through a wisp of steam. "I think I'll take my coffee with me to the hospital. Who knows, maybe I'll see y'all over there."

Michael turned and walked outside. Hank watched through the living room window as Michael drove away and then let the curtain fall back into place.

"Abby, maybe it's better if we don't spend so much time together."

"That would make Michael happy. But I want to help."

"I don't think that's a good idea. Besides, if you got involved, you could get hurt. I appreciate that Facebook thing you showed me, but I'll take it from here."

"Even social engineering?"

"I don't think I'll be doing any of that."

"A woman can find out things a man can't, just by talking to people."

The garage door opened and closed, prompting Hank and Abby to walk to the kitchen. Paul stepped inside from the garage, holding Hank's father's lever action Marlin. Abby rushed to Paul and hugged him just as he leaned the rifle against the doorframe.

"It's so good to see you! Did you get a deer?"

"No. I saw a bunch of squirrels. That's it."

"I'm so relieved," Abby said. "I really didn't want to see a dead deer."

Paul turned to face Hank. "We're going to go shoot some targets down at the gully."

"I didn't realize that's what y'all had planned," Hank said.

"Well," Paul replied, "you've been pretty busy with your workshop."

I've been busy with something or other for most of Paul's life. "When are you going to the hospital to see your Mom?"

"Later this evening."

"Call Willie before you start shooting."

"Wilco," Paul responded. Hank felt a mix of pride and disappointment whenever Paul used military terms in normal conversations. He had never wanted Paul to join the military.

"What kind of rifle is that?" Abby asked.

"It's a Marlin 336," Paul said.

"It looks like a cowboy gun," she said.

Paul grinned. "We won't be shooting this one. I'll teach you how to shoot the M1 Carbine this morning. It's a good starter rifle."

Hank had become a spectator to Paul and Abby's conversation, so he crept upstairs and grabbed his coat. Paul had grown into a fine young man, he thought, even though he had been absent for half of Paul's life.

When Hank came back down to the kitchen, Paul and Abby were talking in the living room, so he pulled the address book from the drawer beside the garage door. He opened it to JD's number and dialed as he walked out through the living room. Paul and Abby nodded at him but said nothing. Hank glanced at the photos in the foyer on his way out the front door, part of him hoping that JD would not answer, but he did.

"Happy Thanksgiving, JD."

"Hank? Well, isn't this a nice surprise. Happy Thanksgiving to you, too, little brother."

"How's Kelly and the girls?"

"They're doing well. But there's lots of drama when you're raising girls, I'll tell you what."

"Yeah, well, I'm learning a little bit about drama myself, thanks to Michael. There's this girl who's been helping me."

"Helping you what?"

"Track down the shooter."

"You said 'girl.' How old is she?"

"She's almost 21," Hank said, and then cringed at the wording of his response.

"So, is she in the Army, or in college or something?"

"College, but she's also a singer."

"A twenty-year-old singer? And she's helping you track down a killer?"

"Her uncle was a cop," Hank said. As soon as he'd said it, he realized how inane that sounded. He started the truck while waiting for JD's response.

"It takes all kinds, I guess. One of the best cops I ever knew was a woman who had been a schoolteacher for a couple of years before she put on a badge."

"Yeah," Hank said, relieved. "It takes all kinds."

"Is she attractive?"

"Average, I guess. She's a sweet girl. I thought for years that she and Paul—"

"Is she attracted to you?"

"I'm old enough to be her father, JD."

"That's not what I asked. I've seen improper relationships develop, especially when a young female cop is partnered with an older male. Even when their relationship doesn't become sexual, it can cross some emotional boundaries."

"Yeah. I can see how that would happen with partners, but we're not cops. We're just occasional collaborators. The thing is, she and my friend Pete are the only ones helping me."

"*I'm* helping."

"That's debatable."

"All right then. Accept her help but maintain your boundaries. Tell me about your friend Pete."

"Pete was ... a cook in the Army. He retired and opened a restaurant."

"A singer and a cook," JD chuckled. "That's quite a team you're putting together."

Hank bristled at the comment. "Pete was a cook in a *Ranger* battalion. Before that, he was a mechanic. He saw combat in Grenada, Panama, and Somalia. And he wasn't *just* a cook, he's done some other stuff, too. Besides, they're my friends. And they're willing to help when others won't."

"No disrespect intended. Like I said, it takes all kinds. But you didn't just call about Pete and that girl, did you?"

"No," Hank admitted.

"So, about this detective you mentioned in your email. I was hoping I had a contact up that way that you could confide in. The bad news is I checked around, and I don't know anybody in the Fayetteville PD. I don't have any contacts in the Cumberland County Sheriff's Office, either."

"So, what's the good news?" Hank asked.

"A couple of years back, I attended a training course down at Glynco. I met this awesome guy from the North Carolina State Police named Matt Grogan. We've stayed in touch. He's on the Anti-terrorism Task Force, so he's not involved in ordinary crime. He's a straight shooter, but he's all about doing whatever it takes to bust the bad boys. You can talk to him if you need a confidant, but if you do anything illegal, don't expect any help from him. Like I said, he's a straight shooter."

23

That night, when Iqbal entered his apartment, he found Bilal playing *Call of Duty*. An empty teacup and two Diet Coke cans lay on the coffee table beside him.

"What have you been up to today?" Iqbal asked over the din of combat that blared from the television.

Bilal paused his game. "Trying to stay alive in this game. Did you enjoy your dinner?"

"Yes."

"I can't believe you went to Thanksgiving dinner with a Christian family. We are supposed to be mujahidin."

"Sometimes the best mujahid is one who is not suspected of being a mujahid."

"Did you drink wine?"

"One glass, yes."

"Hmm," Bilal grunted and gave Iqbal a blistering look. "Listen, I've been thinking. I should have gone into the store instead of Jamal."

"Perhaps you'd be in jail now if you had," Iqbal responded.

"No," Bilal said. "I would have covered the store properly."

"You don't know what might have happened," Iqbal said. "You might have shot that man who was hiding in the cooler."

"Yes. I probably would have, as well as the clerk. That store sells alcohol and sex magazines, so those men deserved to die. I sometimes think I'm not trusted."

"At this point, we need to focus on training and on not getting arrested," Iqbal replied.

"Yes. But does that mean that we will always be mere lookouts?"

"In the long term, men with clean skins are more valuable," Iqbal said. "So, keep your skin clean and be patient. Now, I would like to go to sleep."

"I did not join the jihad to be a lookout for those Egyptian boys from Charlotte," Bilal said. "Did you know they are both high school dropouts? Yet we were made to be lookouts. I want to go inside on the next op."

"If there *is* a next one, you mean. Besides, I get the feeling we're just expected to follow instructions at this stage."

"Yes, just follow instructions," Bilal said. "Instructions are not the same as *duty*."

Iqbal said nothing as he tossed his jacket on the sofa. He walked to the refrigerator and poured himself a glass of milk.

"By the way, my father called again this evening," Bilal said from the living room.

"So, did you argue again?" Iqbal asked.

"No, I didn't answer. Do you know why?"

"Why, Bilal?"

"Because I'm tired of being told to follow instructions."

24

Hank stopped his truck outside Abby's apartment, and she hopped in, sporting a girlish grin, an old pair of jeans and a flannel shirt. She clutched a small purse and a notebook.

"What's the game plan?" she asked.

"We are just going to go talk to some people."

"What people?"

"Mostly convenience store workers. Over the last couple of days, I built a database of convenience store robberies in Eastern North Carolina. Then I identified those similar to the one I witnessed. I plotted those on a map. Then came the hard part. I looked for convenience stores and similar businesses that had not been robbed recently but had a lot of the same characteristics. Those are the most likely next targets. We're going to pay them a visit before the bad guys do."

"Where do we start?"

"Based on my analysis," Hank said, "he's likely to hit one of the convenience stores along Highway 401 north of downtown or one of the shops a few blocks off the highway. So, we need to go by the print shop and pick up the business cards."

"What?"

"You know the print shop where I got the map printed? I also ordered business cards. The business cards will help us set up a reporting network. If this were a tactical intelligence problem, I'd coordinate for intelligence collection on likely avenues of approach, that sort of thing. But our only intelligence collectors are the people who work in the stores. They will be our reporting net."

"So, we give the employees of those stores our business cards and ask them to call us?"

"Actually, we talk to the managers," he explained. "It's like anything else in business. We need to get the managers to buy into this. If they don't want us talking to their employees, we don't talk to their employees. Besides being unethical, that might cause them to call the Fayetteville PD. Anyway, I'm estimating that with five stores, odds are that three or four managers will buy into what we're doing, and one or two won't. But that's what we have to work with. Once we get the managers to buy in, we sensitize the employees to pre-incident indicators. We do that because it won't do us any good to visit a store after it's been robbed. Analysis after a robbery is history. Intelligence is about what happens next."

An hour later Hank opened a box of business cards that read, "Hank McCaskill, Crime Analyst." In the top left corner, a logo depicted a hand holding a magnifying glass. A large eye peered through it.

"Why don't the cards say, 'Investigator?'" Abby asked.

"Because I am not a licensed investigator, and I don't want to deceive anybody."

"All right. But, seriously, Hank, that logo is really *cheesy*,"

"Indeed," he said, smiling. "Sometimes it pays to appear cheesy."

"Yeah," she said with a roll of her eyes.

"We need to make a good pitch to the managers, and we need to give good briefings to sensitize the employees on what to look for. After that - and *only* after that - do we present the business cards."

"I still think the cards look cheesy."

"Okay. Let's suppose that the cops or, even worse, the shooter, were to get our business cards. I *want* them to underestimate us. As long as the employees are willing and able to call, it's all right for the cards to look *cheesy*."

Their first stop was a convenience store on Highway 401, just two miles south of the store where Sabine had been shot. Hank approached the cashier, a muscular, clean-cut man in his early twenties.

"Excuse me," Hank started, but stopped when he felt Abby's hand on his shoulder.

"Good afternoon," Abby said. "Is your manager here?"

"He is," the man said, giving her a wide smile, "but he's in the office. He won't talk to salespeople without an appointment."

"That's all right," she said, "because we're not selling anything. Can you call him to the front? We offer a free service he may be interested in."

"A free service? Well, sure," the man answered. He looked Abby up and down. "As a favor to you, I'll call him. My name's Aidan, by the way."

Abby glanced back at Hank and winked. "Nice to meet you, Aidan. Are you in the Army?"

"Yeah," Aidan said. He leaned across the counter and flexed both arms. "This is my part-time job. I'm a paratrooper. Full time. Eighty second Airborne."

"I should have known. You're in awfully good shape for a cashier," Abby said.

Aidan said nothing, but he looked her up and down and back up again.

"Can I help you?" someone said from behind Hank. He turned to see a plump, middle-aged black man extending his hand.

Hank shook the man's hand and slipped him a business card. "Hank McCaskill, U.S. Army, retired."

"Afternoon, Mr. McCaskill. Jeremy Blackwell. Pleased to meet you."

"Mr. Blackwell, this is my associate, Ms. Mercer. We are crime analysts."

"What?" Mr. Blackwell asked.

"Crime analysts. We look for patterns of criminal behavior and try to help businesses and law enforcement get ahead of the problem."

"Um, all right. What kind of crimes are you analyzing in my store?"

"Oh, it's not *in* your store, Mr. Blackwell, it's *around* your store. We'd like to talk to you about a string of robberies," Hank said.

"Another one? Oh no," Mr. Blackwell said, shaking his head.

"Actually, this is a robbery that hasn't happened yet," Hank said.

Mr. Blackwell squinted at Hank. "Okay, tell me more."

"There's been a string of robberies, which you probably know something about already."

"Yeah. I keep up with the news, and I always talk to the police when they come in here. There's a patrol cop named Murray that I talk to pretty regularly."

"Good, then this won't take long. This particular robber likes to stake out a place carefully and disable the security camera before he strikes."

"All right, so what do you want from me?"

"Very simple, Mr. Blackwell. I want your cashiers to call me immediately if your security camera is disabled. Likewise, I'd like for them to call me if they suspect the store is being staked out."

"Easy enough. But why should I call you instead of the police? And what do you charge?"

"We're not charging you anything," Abby said. "We're working for a client who has an interest in stopping this string of robberies."

"I see," Mr. Blackwell said, but he still looked at Hank and Abby warily.

"I'm not asking you to call us *instead* of the police," Hank added.

"I'm asking you to call us *in addition* to calling the police. The police may come by to check on your store occasionally, but they don't have the manpower to put your store under surveillance."

"We do," Abby added.

"We *might*," Hank said with a stern glance at Abby.

"So, you want my permission to put my store under surveillance? And you want my employees to call you if the security camera is disabled? And someone else is paying for your services? Sort of like Batman and Robin. Is that it?"

"Um, not exactly, but the most important thing to us — to our client — is that you let me know when the robber is still doing his reconnaissance," Hank said.

Mr. Blackwell nodded in understanding. "Tell you what, Mr. McCaskill," he said, squinting at the business card. "I'll make sure the cashiers know what to look for, and I'll make sure they know to call me immediately if the security camera is disabled."

"Thank you, but—"

"There's just one thing. I want to be the one who calls you, Mr. McCaskill. I don't want my employees to call you or your assistant directly." Mr. Blackwell glanced back at Aidan, the young paratrooper standing behind the cash register. "Is that understood?"

"It's your store, but please, if they can't reach you, would you have them call me?"

"Yeah, I suppose I can do that."

Hank thanked him and shook his hand again. He and Abby turned to leave.

"Goodbye, Ms. Mercer," Aidan called out. "I hope to see you again real soon. I work Tuesdays and Thursdays."

Mr. Blackwell shot Aidan a look as Hank and Abby climbed into Hank's truck.

"This gumshoe routine, it's trickier than it looks in the movies," Hank said.

"Yeah, but it will get easier as we go along," Abby said.

A quick motion caught Hank's eye. He turned to see Aidan waving at Abby with one hand and holding up his phone in the other.

"I predict we'll get at least one call from this store," Hank said, "even if it's just lover-boy there looking for a date. This could have gone a little better."

"It could have gone a lot worse," she replied. "They agreed to call us."

"I suppose. Anyway, our next stop is The Steam Room. We've got the home court advantage this time."

When Hank and Abby walked into The Steam Room, they were greeted by the pregnant woman who had been working the night of Abby's concert.

"Good afternoon, ma'am," Hank said. "I'm Hank McCaskill and this is my associate, Abby Mercer."

"Good afternoon. I'm Katrina. Y'all selling something or do you want coffee?"

"Coffee," Hank said. "I'll have an Americano, room for cream."

"Same for me," Abby said.

"You played here a couple of weeks ago, didn't you?" Katrina asked.

"Yes, I did. You were working that night, but I didn't know if you'd remember."

"Of course, I remember! Y'all rocked. We hope y'all play here again soon."

"Maybe after Christmas. With exams and the holidays coming up, I doubt we'll be playing another gig until late January."

"Too bad. I'll have to quit before then."

"I don't mean to pry, but when are you due?" Abby asked.

"About three weeks."

"At three weeks, you could go any time now, right?" Hank asked.

Katrina laughed and rubbed her belly. "Oh yeah," she said over her shoulder as she measured the coffee grounds and juggled the espresso cups.

"Why are you still working?" Abby asked.

"We needed some extra money, especially with the baby coming. But I also enjoy talking to the people who come in here. My husband is deployed, but he's supposed to be back in about two weeks. It's gonna be down to the wire whether he gets home in time."

"Do you have a bag with the necessary supplies nearby, just in case?" Hank asked.

"Of course," Katrina said as she slid their coffees across the counter. She gave Hank a sideways glance.

"Katrina," Abby said, "I'm sorry you have to work so close to your due date, but there's something Hank and I would like to talk to you about. It's about the coffee shop. Is your manager here?"

"Are we in trouble with the Health Department again?" Katrina asked.

Hank peered into his coffee and frowned. "No," he replied. "There's been a string of armed robberies, probably committed by the same man, and we're concerned he might rob your shop soon. We'd like to talk to your manager."

"Good luck with that. Our manager works about twenty hours a week and doesn't answer his phone most of the time." Katrina said. With a dismissive snort, she added, "His dad owns the place."

"All right then. If you work evenings, a robbery may occur while you're here."

"Good luck with that, too. We don't keep much cash on hand. Most people pay with plastic."

Hank slid his business card across the counter. "Still, here's my business card." Without asking, Abby intercepted the card and wrote her phone number on the back.

"I want you to call me immediately if you see anything suspicious," Hank said.

"And if you'd rather talk to a woman, you can call me," Abby added. She gave Hank a smug grin.

"So, y'all are Crime Analysts," Katrina said. "That sounds really interesting. What's your definition of suspicious? Like, a construction worker ordering a spiced chai soy latte?"

"No," Hank said, laughing. "We're looking for *the presence of the abnormal* or *the absence of the normal.*"

"Okay, but what specifically?"

"Specifically, we're interested if your external security camera is disabled, or if you see anyone watching the coffee shop. If it's our guy, he'll pay attention to the counter, probably try to see what's behind it. Do you have an alarm button under the counter?"

"What?"

"An alarm button, a button to push in case you need to call 9-1-1," Abby said.

"No, we don't have anything like that," Katrina said.

"Please talk to your manager and have him call me. Installing an alarm button would be a prudent security measure."

"If it involves spending money on the shop, it ain't gonna happen," Katrina said.

"Too bad he doesn't want to invest more in his shop. This coffee is really good," Hank said before squinting at the menu board. "I'd like to get a large black coffee to go, but I can't see how much it costs from here." When Katrina turned her back to look behind her, he slipped two twenty-dollar bills into her tip jar.

Hank and Abby climbed back into his truck, Hank holding a large to-go cup of coffee that he did not want. "The gumshoe routine was a little easier this time, but it was also more expensive."

Before Abby could reply, Hank's phone rang. When he saw that it was Ballinger, Hank got a bad feeling, but he answered anyway.

"Good afternoon, Detective Ballinger. What's up?"

"There's a development I want to talk to you about."

"Excellent. I'm all ears."

"You probably ought to come to the station for this."

Hank felt uneasy, but he responded, "All right. I'm downtown this afternoon. I can be there in about fifteen minutes."

"See you in fifteen," Ballinger replied. He ended the call before Hank could say anything further.

Inside the third floor of the station, Hank wound his way through a maze of cubicles and then sat in an ancient, gray metal chair in front of Ballinger's desk. Ballinger was on the phone, but he nodded to acknowledge Hank's presence.

As Hank waited, anticipating new information about Sabine's shooter, he studied the photos and awards that adorned the cubicle. He learned that Ballinger had been a Security Policeman in the Air Force and had won several awards as a detective in Fayetteville. The awards were centered around two framed newspaper front pages. One had the headline "Raeford Man Convicted in Murder of Fayetteville Entrepreneur." The other read "Cold Case Reopened and Solved."

Ballinger hung up and examined Hank as if surveying an ugly crime scene. "So, how's business for Fayetteville's newest crime-fighting duo?"

"Excuse me?" Hank asked.

"One of our beat cops called in a little while ago. Name's Murray. He's good friends with a convenience store owner named Jerry Blackwell."

"*Jeremy* Blackwell," Hank replied.

"Whatever. Anyway, *Mister* Blackwell showed Murray a business card with your information on it. Said you were some sort of private investigator but preferred the title 'Crime Analyst.'"

"Yes. Crime Analyst. That's what I'm doing in my spare time these days."

"Right. So, Murray calls dispatch. Dispatch calls the desk sergeant. Desk sergeant asks around about a Hank McCaskill. Few minutes later, the desk sergeant calls me. And a few minutes after that, I call you. Now, uh, here you are."

"Yes. Here I am."

"So, you're Batman and your girlfriend is Robin? Is that it?"

Hank felt his anger rising and his blood rushing to his face. He knew that Ballinger might find out about his and Abby's canvassing local stores, but he hadn't thought it would happen so quickly. Ballinger's lips curled into a faint smile. Ballinger was deliberately provoking him. Even worse, it was working. If this was to be an adversarial conversation, Hank needed to gain the initiative.

"Detective, I'm only here because you said there was a development you wanted to talk about. What information do you have for me?"

"Nada. In fact, I don't think I'll have much information for you at all unless we make an arrest."

"Did you mean to say *until* you make an arrest?"

"No. Now listen here, I know you're angry because your wife was shot, but we don't need any of your vigilante stuff mucking up this investigation, maybe tainting evidence. Tainted evidence can be worse than no evidence."

"What are you doing to catch the man who shot my wife?"

"Everything I can. Now, if you want me to catch him, Mr. McCaskill, cut out the amateur detective stuff. Stay out of this unless I call you."

"You mind if I speak to your supervisor about this?"

Ballinger did not answer. Instead, he picked up the phone on his desk and punched in a number.

"Hey, Larry, it's me. Sorry to bother you, but I got an unhappy customer at my desk. Oh yeah. The one I told you about."

Moments later, a clean-cut middle-aged man in a good suit introduced himself as Lieutenant Larry Snyder. He stood uncomfortably close to Hank's chair, so Hank did not stand. Larry listened and looked down at Hank while Ballinger described the situation.

Hank tuned out the words but could not help bristling every time Ballinger uttered the phrase "amateur detective." Hank had worked in bureaucracies long enough to know that he was being placated about the past, sent on his way in the present, and warned about the future. He stood abruptly, his anger turning into rage.

"Which way is your captain's office?" Hank growled.

Both men looked shocked, but Lieutenant Snyder regained his composure first. "Let me save you a walk, Mr. McCaskill." He picked up the phone on Ballinger's desk and hit a button.

"Hey Belinda," he said, "this is Larry. Is the captain busy? Yeah, I can wait for two minutes."

Hank concentrated on controlling his breathing and his blood pressure. He looked at Lieutenant Snyder, expecting him to speak, but the lieutenant said nothing. All three men stood without speaking for about two minutes, listening to the police bureaucracy chugging along in the surrounding cubicles. Hank felt his anger coming under control, and he thought about his next move, which did not involve talking to a police captain.

"Let me save you a wait, Lieutenant," Hank said as he sat back down.

"Belinda," Larry said into the phone, "never mind. I'll see the captain later today. Take care."

"Anything else, Derek?" Larry asked Ballinger, but he stood uncomfortably close to Hank's chair again. He glared down at Hank as he spoke.

"No, boss," Ballinger replied. "I think I got this."

Hank watched Larry walk away and then turned to Ballinger. "There's nothing illegal about what I'm doing."

"No, but it ain't very helpful, now, is it?"

"You wouldn't know. You haven't accepted my help."

"Do both of us a favor. Now that you're retired, find a hobby. I recommend fishing."

"That would make Pete happy, but my hobby these days is being a crime analyst. And we need to help each other, not argue about roles."

"Agreed. And *you* can help *me* by not interfering with my investigation."

At least it was out in the open now. Hank needed to gain Ballinger's cooperation, or at least his neutrality, and being confrontational would not help. On the other hand, he could not afford to do nothing, and he could not tolerate being sidelined.

Hank thought about disclosing what he knew about how Jamal Wilson had died but thought better of it. That was an ace he could play later. He decided on a softer approach.

"It was never my intent to interfere. Quite the opposite, in fact."

"I told you I'd keep you updated. Okay?"

"It was never my intent to cause you any headaches, either. I just want justice, and I know I can help you get it." Hank stood, feeling calm and focused.

"Look," Ballinger said, "we see this a lot. Your wife was the victim of a violent crime. You want to do something, and in your case, you got some relevant skills. But doctors don't operate on family members. Same thing here. Even cops shouldn't investigate crimes against their own families, and you're not even a cop. Now, do us both a favor. No vigilante stuff, no playing detective. Find something else to do with your time. I recommend fishing."

As soon as Hank climbed back into the truck, Abby asked about the new development.

"The new development is that Ballinger wants me to stop interfering with his investigation."

"You're not interfering."

"Ballinger thinks otherwise," Hank said. "And he's the detective."

"So, what are you going to do?"

"I have two courses of action. I can play it safe and let the local police handle it, or I can play with fire. But first, I'm going to do some time-series analysis of my data to check out a hunch. If my hunch is right, I'll take my analysis to Isaac."

"Who's Isaac?"

"Isaac is not a person. I-S-A-A-C is the Information Sharing and Analysis Center. It's the North Carolina State Police's intelligence arm. My brother JD has a friend up there."

25

Hank sat in a lobby of the state police office, which lay nestled halfway up a Raleigh high-rise. He ignored the view of the city to his left and the ocean blue carpet beneath his feet. Instead, he tapped a foot in rhythm with the classical guitar music on the sound system. He balanced his laptop on his knees and studied his Excel spreadsheets and charts for the hundredth time. He took a deep breath and rehearsed his opening statements. When he was done, he glanced at the clock on the wall. *Still two minutes to go.*

At 9:30 AM, a heavy wooden door swung open, and two men emerged. The first man was medium-framed, about fifty, and sported a brushy head of granite-gray hair that matched his eyes. His shirtsleeves were rolled halfway up his scarred, muscular forearms. The second man was a slender, thirty-something fellow wearing a purple shirt and dark slacks. His clothes contrasted with his pale skin, making him resemble a skinny penguin.

The gray-haired man extended his hand. "Mr. McCaskill, I'm Special Agent Grogan and this is Chad Manigault. He's one of our analysts."

Hank stood, tucked his laptop under his left arm, and shook their hands. Agent Grogan studied Hank while Chad forced a smile.

Hank noted both Grogan's visual examination and Chad's forced smile. "I appreciate your taking the time to meet me," Hank said.

Chad handed Hank's driver's license to him. "Your security clearance checks out, Mr. McCaskill," he said.

"So, JD is your brother, huh?" Grogan asked.

"Yes. Can't you see the resemblance?"

"Absolutely, but he's a good bit taller. How's JD doing?"

"Retired and living in the country."

"Good for him. I hope to do the same in a few years." Grogan said. "He said you just retired from the Army. How long were you in?"

"Twenty-six years."

Grogan whistled. "Thank you for your service. I served in the Marine Corps for six, and that was enough for me. Not like I had much of a choice," he added. "I have an older brother, so, in my family, it was the priesthood or the Corps for me."

Hank chuckled, encouraged that he might have met a kindred soul. He could not quite place Grogan's faint accent. It might have been Philadelphia, but Grogan spoke like a man raised in the northeast and transplanted to the south.

"Well, you *did* have a choice about meeting me," Hank said.

"JD said your wife had been shot," Grogan said. "Then, when you called, you sounded like you knew what you were talking about with the analytics. Chad and I reserved a conference room for an hour." He motioned to the heavy wooden door. "Any cell phones or weapons on you?"

"No. Left them in the car."

"Wireless on your laptop?"

"It's turned off."

Grogan led Hank to a small conference room behind the first door on the left, which told Hank this was where Grogan interviewed people who had no business knowing the layout of the entire floor.

"Coffee, Mr. McCaskill?" Grogan asked, as Hank sat and opened his laptop.

"Please. Black. And call me Hank."

Chad sat beside Hank while Grogan poured three cups of coffee. "Let's see what you got," Grogan said, after settling into the chair at the end of the table.

"As you know," Hank said, "most crime reports are made public on law enforcement websites. So, I built a database using publicly available information on crime in Eastern North Carolina. Because different departments use different formats, I had to do a lot of normalizing data and standardizing formats—"

"What kind of hardware are you running?" Chad asked.

"Alienware. This bad boy supports all the latest games. I just keep it in a travel case so the alien head logo won't attract attention. It can also support ArcGIS mapping software, video processing, everything. One of my soldiers — one of my *former* soldiers — is really good with computers. He helped me set it up. It will take just a second for the map to pop up."

"Intelligence officer, huh?" Grogan said. "Back when I was in the Corps, our intel guys studied maps until their eyeballs bled."

"I still do," Hank said.

Grogan and Chad scooted closer as Hank adjusted the zoom. Soon, the map filled the screen. "These dots on the map represent discreet events — crimes — that I was able to track from publicly available information. Then I used kernel density analysis. I assigned a numerical value to each robbery, based on its resemblance to the one I witnessed in person. Then I used an Excel-to-GoogleEarth conversion tool to color-code the crime locations in accordance—"

"What does your map show me?" Grogan asked.

"Right now, it shows two years of armed robberies in Cumberland County and the adjacent counties."

Hank's fingers clattered on the keyboard. "This next map is a simple choropleth map, what people sometimes call a heat map, although I really hate that term and so do most of the analysts I work with."

Hank looked at Chad, who smiled and nodded.

"The various colors represent density of calls-for-service, which is a standard metric in crime analysis. You'd expect more robberies in high-crime areas. But this group is mobile and selective. So, I focused on robberies that are *not* in high-crime areas."

"Why'd you do that?" Grogan asked.

"Because these are not ordinary armed robbers. You'll see in a bit. That leaves us with these robberies here." Hank's fingers danced, and the choropleth map disappeared, along with most of the dots. "I whittled the list down further by looking only at robberies close to major roads. That was based on the likelihood that the robberies were conducted by a mobile team using two cars. That's how they operated the night my wife was shot."

Grogan shot Chad a glance.

Again, Hank typed, and again, the number of dots dwindled. He minimized the map and pulled up a photograph. "I downloaded Google Maps imagery of each location where this group may have conducted a robbery. The night my wife was shot, the robber fled on foot, but I don't think this group flees to a house or to a common location. I think they flee to cars parked nearby, but beyond the range of any security cameras. They use their cars as their 'Objective Rally Points,' if you want to use military terms."

"You think they use more than one car?" Grogan asked.

"Based on my observation of one crime scene, I think so, but I'm not certain. One getaway car and one lookout car. This gang has a strong aversion to security cameras, and that is the biggest limiting factor on where they park their getaway cars. They need a place far enough away to avoid being recorded, but close enough to enable a quick getaway. That led me to a list of viable targets. I then focused on their target selection criteria. I rated each viable target on three factors: isolation of employees, the difficulty involved in disabling the security camera, and, most important, ease of access to their getaway cars."

"I'm with you," Grogan said.

"I came up with these five businesses here as their most likely next targets," Hank said, pointing to the map. "Then I sensitized the employees at two of the five locations on what to look for and how to report. That's my reporting net." He looked at Grogan and Chad.

Chad smiled, and Grogan studied Hank's face. "That's good work, Hank," he said. "But I still don't see any connection with terrorism."

Hank beamed. "The real prize is the day-of-the week analysis. It's pretty basic compared to what a serious data analyst could do, but it's helpful."

"What do you mean?" Grogan asked.

Hank turned the laptop back to face him and pulled up a tab of the spreadsheet. "The top five robberies that most closely matched the one I interrupted have one thing in common." He waited for a response.

"And that is?" Grogan asked.

Hank turned the laptop around. "They all occurred on a Friday."

"All right," Grogan said. "Why is that significant?"

"Osama bin Laden and his right-hand man Zawahiri issued a fatwa in 1998 that amounted to a declaration of war. That fatwa stressed that it was acceptable to attack America and Americans anywhere and anytime. Some of his followers have interpreted the 1998 fatwa to mean that Friday is the best day of the week to conduct an attack. Their reasoning is that any good Muslim would be in a mosque or at home on Friday. It's their way of limiting collateral damage."

"They all happened on a Friday. *That's* your terrorism connection?" Chad asked.

"So, you're saying they're terrorists, but they rob convenience stores?" Grogan asked.

"Not exactly," Hank said, his voice rising in pitch. "I think they're terrorist wannabes."

"Okay," Chad said. "Maybe these *terrorist wannabes* hit on Friday nights because that's when the stores have the most cash on hand."

"Not at all. In fact, convenience stores usually have the most cash right after they change registers out every afternoon. On Friday evenings, they usually have little cash in the drawer. A lot of Friday customers get cash back with their purchases, which depletes the cash on hand. Friday night is actually the least profitable time to rob a convenience store. I found that out by talking to a convenience store clerk."

Grogan nodded while Chad knotted his brow.

"It's some good work," Grogan said. "But I gotta be honest with you, Hank. The terrorism connection is weak. You suspect a group of robberies were committed by the same gang because of common factors. You suspect they have a terrorist connection because they all occurred on Fridays. But State can't act on any of this. And why didn't you take this to the local PD first?"

Hank felt his plan deflating, but he kept his composure. "Let's just say I don't have a good relationship with the Fayetteville PD."

"Sorry to hear that," Grogan said, "but that explains why you brought it to us. With your background, you should have known I was going to ask."

"Then why didn't you ask right away?" Hank asked.

"We wanted to see what you had, for one thing," Chad answered. "For another, our Fusion Center produces similar products that are a lot more sophisticated, but it's always helpful to get a fresh perspective, so I wanted to meet you."

"Hank," Grogan said, "you're a smart guy. You had to know we're obligated to share with local law enforcement."

"Yes, but I thought it would be more authoritative if this came from you."

"Like I said, this is some good work, and I hope you continue crunching away at it. It's just that I've got no desire to raise the alarm with Fayetteville's PD over somebody else's hunch."

Disappointment washed over Hank like an icy wave.

Chad pursed his lips. "All of your hypotheses are possible, based on your data, but you don't have anything conclusive. And your data is just publicly available crime data. We work with more accurate and detailed databases here. I mean, what you showed us is intriguing, and we'll look into it, but it's not actionable."

"It's not actionable *yet*," Hank said.

Chad procured a USB stick from his shirt pocket. "If you'll let me see your computer, I'll copy your spreadsheet and compare it to some of our analytical products."

Hank felt a chill. "Not yet," he said. "I, um, still need to clean up and standardize some of my data. I can email it to you in a couple of days. When it's closer to being actionable."

Chad's eyes darted toward Grogan. "We don't like to receive anything sensitive via email."

Hank froze, his hand on the laptop, as he considered his options.

Grogan cut his eyes toward Chad. "Just mail us a data stick when you're satisfied with it. Chad and our other analysts can check it out."

Chad extended the USB stick a little closer to Hank. "*Most* of the data sets I draw from are works in progress. I'll be glad to take it now and see what I can tease out of it."

Hank looked from Grogan to Chad and back to Grogan. "Thanks, but I'll hold on to it until I clean it up."

Chad withdrew the USB stick and dropped it into his shirt pocket. He looked both amused and irritated.

Grogan's mouth smiled, but his eyes did not. "Hank, I appreciate your bringing this to us. It's just not anything we can roll with. But ..." Grogan held his hands palm upward and hesitated.

"But what?" Hank asked.

"Look, you're not a nut job, and you're not an amateur. You're onto *something*. I just don't know what it is."

"Neither do I," Hank said.

Grogan stood and extended his hand, indicating that the meeting was over. "Whatever is going on, here's my card. If your analysis leads you to something conclusive — like an impending terrorist plot — call my cell. I don't care what time it is, just call." He motioned toward the door.

"I will," Hank said as he shook Grogan's hand. "Thank you, Agent Grogan. Chad."

"Just save your finished product to a USB stick," Chad added. "I can meet you somewhere and pick it up. Or you can FedEx it. Do *not* email it."

"Deal," Hank said. He shook Chad's hand and noted how soft it was. "Thank you for your time, gentlemen."

Hank left the building in a daze and climbed into Sabine's Escape, only then realizing that his lower back muscles were tightening.

What were his options now? He sat in the car and let his mind work. If he sent the data stick to Chad, and Chad shared it with Fayetteville PD, Ballinger would know he had been talking to state. But if he didn't send it at all, he would look paranoid, and Chad or Grogan would almost certainly call the Fayetteville PD. If that happened, Chad's call would be a warning about Hank rather than a tip about a suspected terrorist group.

Hank started the car and drove toward the parking lot exit, his numb hands gripping the steering wheel. The blare of a car horn interrupted his thoughts. He realized he had been sitting at the parking lot exit for at least a minute. He mouthed, "Sorry," at the rearview mirror and pulled out into traffic.

Neither option was good, but he had a third option. He could do his own surveillance of the three stores that he and Abby had not visited. And that might enable him to disrupt their next robbery.

26

The fickle North Carolina winter turned warm overnight, letting Hank conduct his morning workout with the garage door open. After a quick shower, he went to see Sabine, hoping she had improved, but nothing had changed. Still, he prayed at her bedside, kissed her on the forehead, and tiptoed out of the room. After lunch at Pete's, he spent the afternoon firing his H&K45 and his Ruger Mini-14.

With his hands throbbing and his ears ringing, he ate a light, early dinner of garbanzos and grilled chicken. *Never eat heavy on a surveillance night*, he thought just before he sat down at his computer. There, he puzzled through formulas in Microsoft Excel for thirty minutes before figuring out how to create a chart that depicted a scatterplot of times and dates for armed robberies. Once he figured that out, he highlighted in bright yellow the five robberies he attributed to the same group. This would show Chad the improbability of all of them happening on a Friday night. He saved his finished spreadsheet on a USB stick and dropped it into a FedEx envelope addressed to the state police.

Hank grabbed a can of club soda from the refrigerator, went back to his computer, and pulled up Google Maps. He zoomed in on the three businesses that he and Abby had not visited before Ballinger warned him off. The first was a convenience store that stood beside a McDonald's. Its parking lot was well lit and easily visible from the road. The second was a BP station, also well lit, with at least eight gas pumps and a Subway sandwich shop next door. The third was a small, independent convenience store called Bee's Market. A check cashing business stood on one side, and an empty warehouse stood on the other, its vacant parking lot dotted with weeds. Hank remembered riding past Bee's Market at night. The parking lot and the back of the store were shrouded in shadows.

He switched to Street View and examined the building from several angles, zooming in and out to consider different ranges. Bee's Market consisted of cinder block walls propping up a warped metal roof and a trio of barred, darkened windows. A small parking lot with two non-operational gas pumps obscured the view from the street.

Keeping in mind the terrain around the store where Sabine had been shot, Hank backed out of street view and assessed avenues of approach to the building. Then he checked lines of sight to the parking lot.

"Bee's Market, you're next," he said. He closed his computer, stood, and hefted the black rucksack that held his binoculars, camera, first aid kit, and water. The rucksack was nearly full, but he stuffed a lightweight camouflaged tarp into it anyway. There was one more thing to do before going to set up his observation post.

He set the rucksack down, knelt at his desk, and prayed. *God, lead me to the man who shot Sabine. Please help--*.

Before Hank could finish his prayer, his cell phone rang. Irritated, he reached for it, knocking a crime analysis book to the floor with his fist.

"Mr. McCaskill?" a voice groaned. Hank struggled to identify the voice, closed his eyes for an instant, and imagined a very pregnant, dark-haired lady in a coffee shop.

"Katrina?"

"Yes. Thank God I reached you—"

"I'm sorry, but I've been warned not to play detective. You need to hang up and call the police."

"That's not what I—" she began, but then her voice trailed off into a groan.

Hank stood and started toward his bedroom. "What's wrong?"

"I don't know. I think the baby may be coming early. It hurts, and I feel strange in my head."

"The baby?" Hank said, a little more gruffly than he intended. "All right, Katrina, this is not what I was expecting, but I'll help. Tell me about your situation."

"My situation is it hurts," Katrina groaned, "and I can't reach my husband's rear detachment commander on the phone. My Mom is on the way, but she lives six hours from here. The store manager doesn't answer. Neither does your friend Abby."

Hank tried to remove a shirt from its hanger with the telephone propped between his chin and shoulder. He glanced at the Google Maps imagery of Bee's Market and muttered. His ballistic vest lay on the floor beside the bed, a taunting reminder that helping might quash his best chance of catching the man who shot Sabine.

"All right. Tell me your symptoms." Hank said. It was the same tone he would have used when talking to a sick or injured soldier. He muttered in irritation as he struggled to pull on a casual button-up shirt and keep his ear to the telephone at the same time.

"I just told you my symptoms, Mr. McCaskill. It hurts, and I don't feel right."

"But you're not having contractions?" he asked as he finally wrestled his shoulders into the shirt.

"No."

"Who else is in the shop with you?"

"Right now, nobody, but there's a play at Gilbert Theater tonight, and we'll get a crowd as soon as it lets out."

"All right, I'm not really—"

"Mr. McCaskill?"

"Yes, Katrina?"

"The baby isn't the only thing. About five minutes ago, our security company called. The external security camera quit working."

The phone fell from Hank's shoulder, but he caught it with his left hand as his mind shifted into a higher gear.

"Listen carefully, Katrina, and do exactly what I tell you. Stop what you're doing and go lock the door. Right now."

"Lock the door? But the manager wants me to stay open until after the play."

"Business is slow right now. Do it."

Hank tucked the H&K 45 inside his waistband and donned his boots but left them untied. Then he ripped his shirt off, sending buttons flying, and put on his body armor against his skin. He pulled an oversized gray sweatshirt out of the laundry basket and pulled it on over the vest. Finally, he ran outside and started his truck. Just as he jammed it into reverse, Katrina came back on the line.

"I locked the door, Mr. McCaskill. What do I do — oh, that hurts," she groaned. "I feel dizzy again."

"You have a cordless phone, right?"

"Yes."

"As soon as I hang up, dial 9-1-1. Tell them there's a suspicious man outside the shop."

"You want me to lie to the police?"

"It's not a lie. He's there. You just haven't seen him yet."

"Okay. I'll do it."

Hank glanced at his watch as he sped down the street. "I'll be there in twelve minutes. I'll take you to the hospital. Have a seat in the back, where you're not visible to anyone outside."

Twelve minutes and thirty-seven seconds later, Hank parked his truck a block away from the back of the coffee shop. He leaped out, placed his hand on his H&K, and sprinted to the back door. He pressed his back against the brick wall beside the door and tapped three times. Katrina opened the door, her face bearing a pained expression.

"Lock it behind me," Hank said as he stepped inside.

"The police said they'd send a car over," Katrina said, "but they're not here yet."

"Where's your hospital bag?"

She said nothing, but gritted her teeth as she locked the door. She nodded toward the kitchen. Hank stepped into the kitchen and Katrina groaned again. He looked around for the bag but did not see it.

"Have you started timing the contractions?" Hank asked, even though Katrina had said she was not having contractions. It was a trick question from a man who had assisted his wife through three pregnancies.

"No! I told you I don't think I'm having contractions. I just feel like something's wrong."

"Right. No contractions. Just tell me where your bag is because I don't see it. As soon as I find it, we're going to the hospital."

"It's in the back," she said.

"*Where* in the back?" he asked. He kicked a mop bucket in frustration.

"Under the rack with the paper cups and stuff."

Hank picked up the bag and walked to the storefront, where he put an arm around Katrina to steady her as she hobbled toward the back door. As Hank shifted his weight to help her, the front door shattered behind them. Hank spun around to see a shower of glass shards spilling onto the floor. Then Katrina screamed.

27

A familiar, raspy voice called out, "Don't nobody move!"

Hank slid Katrina off his arm so that she leaned on the counter. He turned slowly toward the front of the coffee shop, his pistol heavy on his hip and his heart pounding.

Two masked men stepped through the front door, and one gestured at Hank with a stainless steel .45. Hank let the baby bag slip from his left hand and fall to the floor. He raised his arms.

"Just play nice, old man," said the man with the raspy voice, "and nobody gets hurt."

Hank slowly raised both hands overhead and stared into the man's blue eyes. Just as on the night Sabine had been shot, the man wore a ski mask, a western shirt, blue jeans, and broken-in work boots. A second man, dressed the same, stood behind him and watched the street. Behind the second man, the door stood ajar, a fist-sized hole in the glass and fragments strewn across the floor.

"Right," Hank said, holding his hands a little higher. Hank thought he saw a flash of recognition in the man's eyes, and he prayed the man would not recognize him.

"Okay, *Katrina*," the man said without taking his eyes off Hank. "I know that this time of night, you got a full bank bag under the register. Open the bank bag and put the cash from the register into it."

Katrina made her way along the counter to the register and pulled the bank bag out from under it. She emptied the cash from the register into the bag and tried to stand upright.

Hank struggled to think clearly and to control his heart rate as Katrina tossed the bank bag to the floor. It landed at the blue-eyed man's feet with a muffled crunch of coins cushioned by cash. He glanced downward at the bag, but his gun stayed sighted on Hank.

"I'm going to pick this up. And when I do, if you try anything, I'll kill both of you."

"She's pregnant, you animal," Hank said.

"I don't care if she's the Virgin Mary. I'll kill both of you."

He leaned down to pick up the bag.

"I know you," Hank growled. His chest was heaving now, and a volcanic rage was welling up inside him. *You're the man who shot Sabine,* he thought, but his trembling lips could not form the words.

The blue-eyed man scooped up the bank bag and looked back at Hank. "Yeah, I got a famous face. They call it a 'ski mask.'"

"Not your face, your voice."

The blue-eyed man's hand tightened on the grip of the .45. "Who are you?"

Hank's eyes widened as he focused on the man's hands. The blue-eyed man's accomplice said something, but Hank could not discern the words. He could only study the hands and pistol pointing at his chest. Before he could reply, Katrina cried out in pain, causing both men to look toward her. The robber kept the gun pointed at Hank as Katrina held her hands together on her lower back again.

"This one's bad," she gasped. "It hurts really bad."

The robber tipped his head to the side. "Get the tip jar, Katrina!"

She pulled her hands away from her lower back long enough to set the tip jar on the counter. When the blue-eyed man didn't move toward it, Katrina picked it up to hand it to him. As Hank watched, the tip jar slipped through her trembling hands, struck the floor, and exploded, sending coins and glass flying.

The blue-eyed man looked down and jumped backward, causing his point of aim to drift from Hank's chest. Hank lunged forward. He covered the six feet between himself and the blue-eyed man, grabbed the man's right wrist with his left hand, and thrust downward with all his strength. He held the man's arm extended, the .45 pointed at the floor. The man squeezed off a round, which ricocheted off the floor and ripped into the counter to Katrina's left. With his right hand, Hank reached underneath his sweatshirt and drew his H&K.

The blue-eyed man must have expected Hank to draw a gun, because he grabbed Hank's right arm with his own left. They struggled, each man grasping the other's gun arm as if dancing. As they struggled, they toppled the chairs and tables in the shop entrance. The blue-eyed man shifted his weight suddenly and head-butted Hank across the bridge of his nose, making a sickening crunch and blurring Hank's vision.

With a sudden twist, the man flung the H&K from Hank's grip and sent it flying across the room. Hank coughed and spat blood, but through his blurred eyesight, he glimpsed the man's throat and seized it with his right hand. When the man knocked Hank's hand away, Hank grabbed the man's ski mask, but instead of peeling it off, he yanked it downward, bending the man's neck and covering his eyes. When the man straightened his mask Hank leaped forward and slammed his knee into the man's belly.

They turned a slow half-circle, another mockery of a dance. Hank slammed his knee into the man's belly two more times, eliciting a grunt with each blow. When he attempted a third knee-strike, the man blocked Hank's thigh with his shin, twisted, and broke free from Hank's grip. Then Hank's right hand found the man's throat again. This time, Hank felt the man's trachea with his thumb. He jabbed inward with all his strength, all the while continuing to batter the man's belly with his knee. The man's pistol slipped from his grasp, but he caught Hank in the jaw with a right cross. Hank lost his grip and felt a flurry of blows striking his face and head, but he felt them only dully, as if he were in a dream.

He caught a glimpse of the man's gun lying on the floor and kicked it, causing it to spin and skitter across the tile and come to rest against the base of the counter. The next thing Hank knew, his right leg was pinned, and he was going down, with the blue-eyed man on top of him. The air burst from Hank's lungs and glass dug into his back, but there was little pain.

"Shoot them, Daood!" the blue-eyed man yelled.

Katrina cried out again as Hank and his opponent rolled around, each trying to gain the upper position. Hank was dimly aware of the broken glass digging into the backs of his legs. He caught a glimpse of the robber's accomplice picking up the bank bag. He bucked and found himself on top again, but then the world spun underneath him, and he landed once again on his back.

"I have the money! Let's go!" the accomplice yelled.

"Shoot them!" the blue-eyed man screamed, his lips almost touching Hank's left ear. Hank felt another flurry of punches to his face, but then he bucked and rolled and found himself on top again. Somehow, he got both his hands around the man's throat this time. Both of his thumbs found the man's trachea this time. Hank leaned down until the top of his head pressed against the blue-eyed man's face and jammed his thumbs inward with all his might.

The blue-eyed man grabbed Hank's wrists and lurched beneath him, but he couldn't break Hank's grip. Hank found himself looking into the man's eyes. Pale blue. And the man reeked of gunpowder. The man's eyes rolled backward and fluttered, but instead of losing consciousness, he seemed possessed by a sudden, almost supernatural strength. He twisted free from Hank's grasp with a growl, flung him aside, and bounded to his feet. Hank scrambled to his feet, too, expecting the man to make a dash for the .45. Instead, he made a dash for the door. As abruptly as he had appeared, the blue-eyed man disappeared out the door and into the darkness, his accomplice close on his heels.

Katrina cried out in pain again, but this time her cry trailed off into a groan. Hank bent over and gasped for air, red spatters of blood dripping from his face onto the black and white tile. A flicker of motion caught Hank's eye. He thought it was his own reflection in the glass until the blue-eyed man aimed a small revolver at him. *Backup piece.*

"Katrina, get down!" Hank yelled. She was halfway to the floor when Hank dove on top of her. The window glass shivered as a round punched through and buzzed past like an angry hornet. The next round made only a muffled pop as it hit the wall behind Katrina and sent up a spray of powdered plaster. Hank felt the next round slam into his side, but he lay there, covering Katrina's body with his own, feeling her every breath. When the next shot came, the round struck Hank's side like an axe blade. He heard two more shots but, through his pain, could not tell where they struck. Had he been hit again?

He rolled to his left, picked up his H&K45, and looked over the sights from a prone position. He saw nothing, but heard footsteps fleeing. Rising to one knee, Hank thought about chasing the blue-eyed man, but the pain in his side froze him in place.

Katrina groaned again behind him. He wanted to give chase, but he also wanted to collapse and close his eyes and rest. He forced himself to stand upright while watching the doorway.

"Katrina! Are you all right?"

She nodded. "I'm okay," she finally replied between sobs.

A series of sharp pains struck the backs of Hank's legs, and he glanced downward at the smears of blood among the scattered coins and broken glass on the floor. His back muscles contracted, forcing him into a kneeling position. *Did a round penetrate my vest?* Pain shot through his side. *Please, God, no.* He held the pistol with his right and ran his left hand under the edges of the vest as he fought a wave of nausea. No blood.

"Are *you* okay?" Katrina asked.

Hank coughed and sputtered. "Never better."

"Is he gone?"

"I think so. We need an ambulance."

Hank felt his adrenaline dwindling and the pain surging back as he knelt against the counter to keep from falling. A searing pain shot through his abdomen as he continued to scan the storefront and the door. He watched for a few moments until another searing pain hit him. This one was centered on his abdomen. *Dear God, please let the cops and the ambulance get here soon.* Another wave of nausea and dizziness washed over him. *What if I'm hit but didn't find the hole?*

"I may pass out," he muttered. "If he comes back after I'm out, take my pistol and shoot him."

Katrina bent over, picked up the blue-eyed man's .45, and struggled until she stood propped up behind the counter, pistol in hand. To Hank's surprise, she held the pistol properly, checked the safety, and said, "I'd rather shoot him with his own gun, Mr. McCaskill."

Hank glanced down at his aching side again. *Still no blood.*

"You know, Katrina," he laughed, "this ballistic vest really works." Another wave of dizziness washed over him and pushed him into a sitting position. He leaned against the counter and realized he was becoming punch-drunk. Sleep beckoned, but he fought it.

Time passed. Flashing blue lights silhouetted two men with badges approaching the door. Hank put his pistol down and leaned his head back just before they stepped inside, weapons drawn. He felt himself slipping into unconsciousness and hoped again that he hadn't been shot.

I'm trying not to die, Sabine. I'm trying.

28

Fayetteville, North Carolina
December 6, 2008

"You look awful, Major," Ballinger said.

Hank raised his head from the hospital bed and struggled to focus on Ballinger's face. Although the swelling around his eyes made focusing difficult, Hank recognized the detective's voice.

"You don't exactly look like a bowl of peaches yourself, Detective," he replied.

Ballinger looked around. "You know, the first time I interviewed you, it was in this hospital."

"I remember."

"But this time, you're the one who's been shot. So, I'll try to make this quick and painless."

"Painless would be good."

"So, Major," Ballinger said, pulling out his pen and Moleskine notebook, "you're not in custody, and I want to focus on the suspects in this case instead of focusing on you, but I have to know something. How did you manage to be at that coffee shop exactly when it was being robbed?"

"I told you already," Hank said as he looked into Ballinger's eyes and tried to gauge his reaction. He could focus just enough to see the anticipation on Ballinger's face, but nothing more. "It's called 'tactical criminal intelligence.'"

"Right," Ballinger said.

"I gathered crime statistics and did some rudimentary pattern analysis. I figured out his target selection criteria and identified likely targets. Then I set up a reporting net and waited for him to make his next move. It's not rocket surgery."

"Yeah. I've been doing this a while. I know what criminal intelligence is. Guys like you try to predict what's going to happen. Guys like me gather evidence to figure out who's responsible for what's already happened. So, let me put this a different way. What is your connection to the men who robbed that coffee shop?"

"You," Hank replied.

"Excuse me?" Ballinger asked. Despite his blurred vision, Hank could see a wary expression on Ballinger's face.

"My connection to these men is through you, Detective Ballinger. I'm trying to help you catch them, but you don't seem to value my assistance."

"All right," Ballinger said. "Let's skip ahead to the subject description."

"You already got that, too, at least for the leader. I didn't get much face time with his accomplice. Anyway, same guy, same raspy voice, same pale blue eyes, but I got a closer look at them this time. You know, if the eyes are truly the windows to the soul, I think this man may not have one."

"Yeah. Anything else?"

"Same style of shirt, different color this time. You know, I don't think he's making a fashion statement. I think he likes snap-up western shirts because he changes clothes right after he does a job and he just rips his shirt off. Did you find a discarded change of clothes nearby?"

"We need to stick to things you actually saw, Major. Now, is there anything else you'd like to add? A different weapon, different watch, that sort of thing?"

"He shot me with his backup piece, not his primary weapon. His primary weapon was a stainless-steel Kimber M1911 with rosewood grips. I liberated that from him, at great personal risk. Did you run it for prints yet? I'd like to know the name of the man who nearly killed me."

"I can't discuss other evidence with you, Major. You're a witness. I just need to know what *you* saw and heard."

"I heard him empty a revolver in my direction. Then I blacked out. That's about it."

"Right."

"Did you get any usable DNA? Did you check under my fingernails while I was out? Did you swab the blood on the floor? Did Katrina tell you that the robber called her by name? How's she doing this morning?"

"Look, Major, I'm not going to comment on an ongoing investigation when you're a witness."

Just then, Dr. Chan stepped into the room. She knocked a second after she stepped inside, making the knock rather pointless.

"So, Mr. McCaskill, how are we feeling today?" she asked.

"Sore. Irritable. Ready to go home."

Dr. Chan glanced at Detective Ballinger. "Detective Ballinger, Fayetteville PD," Ballinger said as he extended his hand. Dr. Chan ignored Ballinger's hand and studied Hank's chart.

"Are you interrogating my patient, Detective?" she asked without looking at him.

"Actually, Doctor, he was interrogating me." With that, Ballinger snapped his Moleskine notebook shut, pocketed his pen, and pivoted toward the door.

"You're making my job difficult, Major," he said, shaking the notebook at Hank for emphasis, "but I still need a statement, so we'll be in touch."

"All right, Mr. McCaskill," Dr. Chan said. She watched Ballinger's back as he walked out of the room. Then she flipped papers on Hank's chart. "You have three cracked ribs and multiple lacerations on the backs of your shoulders and buttocks, seven of which required stitches. You also have extensive bruising on your face, neck, and knuckles. Hmmm. The head x-rays show you don't have any cranial or maxillary fractures, but you probably experienced a minor concussion. You also have a crack in the bridge of your nose. I didn't reset it because your nose has been broken once before, hasn't it?"

"Twice," Hank said.

Doctor Chan shook her head in disapproval. "I can prescribe an anti-inflammatory for the swelling around your eyes, but I'd prefer that you treat the swelling yourself. You need to rest with your head above your body and apply cold packs." She looked up from the chart. "Are your pain medications working?"

"I thought you were here to talk to me about Sabine," Hank said.

Dr. Chan looked back at Hank's chart. "I'm a trauma doctor, Mr. McCaskill. I'm no longer Sabine's primary care physician."

"But doctors talk to each other. How is she really doing?"

"Sabine's condition *is* slowly improving," she said without looking at Hank, "but she's in a persistent coma." She sighed and looked into Hank's eyes. "Even if she wakes, I don't expect she'll ever make a full re-covery. Now, are your pain medications working?"

"Yeah. The physical pain is bearable. What does that mean, she won't fully recover?"

"It means we don't know. She could have anything from a persistent limp to severe cognitive impairment." She softened her words with a sympathetic look. "Mr. McCaskill, I can discharge you tomorrow after-noon if you're urinating regularly by then. Do you have someone who can drive you home?"

"Yeah," Hank said, struggling to keep his swollen eyes open, "my son Michael."

29

Michael drove Hank home from the hospital in silence, his hands gripping the steering wheel of Hank's truck so hard that his knuckles shone white in the darkness. Michael helped his father out of the truck, up the stairs, and to the front door, but Hank waved off additional help. He limped unassisted into the foyer.

"Dad, you're too old to be doing this vigilante stuff."

"Age is just a number. I intend to find that man."

"For God's sake, Dad, just let the police handle it. That's what they get paid for."

Hank wanted to explain what he had done, but a pair of headlights illuminated the front of the house.

"Your ride is here," Hank said. "Tell Chapman I said thanks for giving you a lift. And Michael, thanks for driving me home."

Michael squeezed Hank's shoulder and whispered, "Be careful, Dad."

As soon as Michael climbed into Chapman's car, Hank turned and waved. He tried not to grimace at the pain but failed. When the car was gone, Hank turned to the mirror in the foyer. His face was swollen and barely recognizable. Bruises in the shape of knuckles adorned his cheeks and forehead. Blood trickled from his left nostril. He grunted and stood upright, wincing from the gashes in his back and the cracked ribs in his side.

He kicked the front door shut and listened to the sound echo through his empty house. He hobbled into the garage and looked around at the weights, punching bag, and treadmill as a cold silence settled around him. After taking a flashlight from a kitchen drawer, he walked across the backyard to his tomato patch.

As the faint light fell upon the vines, he saw a few soggy brown tomatoes littering the ground, a tangle of crumpled brown vines draped across them, and clumps of weeds poking up through the soil in mockery. He thought about his crime analysis, now missing one key event, on a data stick upstairs, still not mailed to the state police.

He hobbled back to the garage and returned to his tomato patch with a shovel. After tossing the flashlight aside, he swung the shovel like a club. He yelled out in pain as he beat the first plant into a tangled heap of brown. Then he sank the shovel blade into the dirt, lifted, and hurled a clump of soil and vines across the fence. His shovel caught on the fence as he retrieved it, causing a hot pain to shoot through his left leg.

A tugging sensation followed by wetness alerted Hank that the stitches in his left buttock had pulled loose. Something brushed past the hedges in the side yard, and he turned toward the sound, expecting to find the blue-eyed man. Instead, he saw a neighbor's cat. Hank hissed, and the cat scurried away.

Hank sat cross-legged on the wet grass. He looked at the sandy patches where his sons' feet used to strike the ground beneath a swing set. Although he had hauled the swing set to the dump years before, the backyard had never felt quite right since, and the sandy patches had not yet been overtaken by grass. He hung his head between his knees and looked at the ground beneath him.

After a few minutes, he rose and trudged back inside, where he washed down a pain pill with a half-liter bottle of German beer. He took a bag of frozen peas from the freezer and placed it on the coffee table, and then arranged the pillows on the sofa so he could sleep upright. On impulse, he went back to the refrigerator for a second bottle of beer and chugged it.

The half-empty bottle of Glenmorangie stood on top of the refrigerator as if waving for his attention. *Special occasion.* He took the bottle down, swallowed most of the contents in two gulps, and threw the bottle at the fireplace. The sound of shattering glass echoed through the house. He glanced at the broken glass as he collapsed onto the sofa and then at the bag of frozen peas. He put the bag on his face and remembered that he had taken a pain pill before drinking. Should he force himself to vomit while the alcohol was still in his stomach? Would he wake up? What difference did it make? He leaned his head back and drifted away on a black river of numbness and, for the first time in years, he fell asleep without praying.

EPILOGUE

A sunbeam from the kitchen was warming Hank's face as he opened his eyes. He knew without looking at the clock that it was almost lunchtime. The sound of nailed fingers brushing an acoustic guitar roused him from his opiate and alcohol-induced sleep. Although he could not make out the tune at first, he recognized *"The Garden Song"* as soon as Abby started singing.

He lay on his couch, listening. He turned to see her sitting on the easy chair, smiling. Next, she played an instrumental version of *"Amazing Grace."* He thought of the tomato vines he had crushed and then wondered how she had gotten into the house. When she finished the song, he looked at her and shook his head.

"How did you get in?" he asked.

"You left the front door unlocked. I knocked, but no one answered, so I came in to check on you. I found a broken beer bottle and a bottle of pain pills, but you were breathing, so I knew you weren't dead. Then I noticed the broken whiskey bottle. I figured I had better wake you up."

"Why didn't you let me sleep?"

"You don't need more sleep. You need to go to church, but since you won't go to church, I brought church to you. Now, get up, or I'm going to start singing old gospel hymns."

"Have you been to the hospital?" Hank asked.

"Yes."

"How is Katrina?"

"She and the baby are doing fine. Her husband got in Saturday night. He missed the birth, but he's there now."

"And Sabine?" Hank asked.

"She's moving her hands and making sounds."

"What?" He bolted upright, bringing a fresh wave of pain onto his back and side. He stayed upright anyway. "Did you say she's talking?"

"It's nothing intelligible, but she's making sounds."

"What kind of sounds?"

"Gibberish."

"Maybe. Or maybe German. Please. What sounds did she make?"

"She said something about a 'malt,' and something else about 'sin.' Any idea what that means?"

"No, but knowing Sabine, it means something."

"How long before you're ready to get back in the fight, Hank?"

"Are you kidding? I don't know that I'll ever get back in the fight. Unless you count fighting my tomato patch."

"You might change your mind."

"I don't think so. It's been eleven weeks since Sabine got shot. I did everything I know to find the man who shot her. I gathered the data, studied the patterns, predicted his next move, and found him. Now, all I have to show for my efforts is some cheesy looking business cards, one angry detective, and a couple of cracked ribs. But, by the grace of God, my wife may be coming out of her coma."

"Katrina and her baby are alive because of you."

"No, Abby, they nearly died because of me. I should have just gone in through the front door of the coffee shop, gun in hand. Instead, I snuck in the back because I didn't want to scare the guy off. Subconsciously, I *wanted* a confrontation." He looked at the floor. "I used a pregnant woman as bait to satisfy my own desire for revenge. I should've just let the police handle this from the start."

Hank lay back on the couch, groaned, and covered his eyes with his forearm. He made a sound that was part sobbing and part laughing. "That was an interesting choice of songs, by the way," he said. "So, other than disturbing an old man's rest with hymns and hippie music, what brings you here?"

"I brought you a gift," she said. "I wanted you to be alert when I gave it to you. That's one reason I didn't give it to you back at the hospital."

"A gift, huh? All right." Hank sat up and groaned as a hot pain shot through his side. "Oh, dear God, my ribs!"

Abby placed a small, gift-wrapped box on the coffee table. "You can take a pain pill in a little while, but right now, you need to be alert."

Hank leaned over the coffee table and tugged at the ribbons and paper. After he fumbled his way through opening the box, he held up an Apple iPhone.

"Wow. A new cell phone. You shouldn't have. Seriously, you shouldn't have."

"It's not new. See how the screen is cracked?"

"Oh yeah. Cracked screen. That's a nice touch, but how did it get cracked?"

"You rolled over it when you were fighting with the man who shot you," Abby said.

Hank stared at the iPhone and felt his pulse quicken. He drew a deep breath and grew dizzy at the implications of the gift that Abby had lain before him.

"How?" he asked.

"I got to the coffee shop at the same time as the police. The whole situation was chaotic. You were unconscious. While we were waiting for the ambulance, I found it on the floor. Apparently, it fell out of the man's pocket, along with some Mexican coins. I took the coins, too, in case they have fingerprints on them."

"How did you hide the phone?"

"I didn't. I just turned it off and slipped it into my purse."

"Why didn't you give it to the police?"

"After Detective Ballinger lied to you, why *would* I give it to the police?"

"Good point."

"Anyway, it was easy. When I got home that night, I took out the battery and SIM card. Just to be safe."

"How did you know to take out the battery and SIM card? And who taught you how?"

"Seriously, Hank? Uncle Sean taught me to be careful, you taught me to be inquisitive, and I'm a two-minute Google expert on anything."

"So, this phone hasn't been turned on in two days?"

"That's right. I was afraid he might have one of those 'find my iPhone' apps."

"Wow. Smart girl. *Very* smart girl."

"So, when can we turn it on and see what's in it? I think there's going to be some delicious information inside."

Hank examined the phone. "I don't know about this."

"It's just a phone."

"This phone is evidence from a crime scene. It's not something we should toy with."

"The information on this phone will lead us to the man who shot Sabine."

"This phone could also land us in prison," Hank said. "Or worse."

Abby leaned up and away from Hank. "Seriously? Ballinger lied to you about the man who shot Sabine. And you think we should just give him the phone?"

"Keeping it would be evidence tampering," Hank said. "Maybe even obstruction of justice."

"This is, like, the biggest break ever, and you just want—"

"I just want to keep *you* safe from harm. Thank you for bringing it to me. I'll find a way to get it to the police anonymously. Or maybe I'll walk down to the river and throw it in. I don't know yet."

"I don't believe this," Abby said. "I don't believe *you*." She cased her guitar and stormed out, leaving the front door open. Hank watched through the open door as she climbed into her car and turned the key. The engine turned and then made a series of rapid clicks. Hank stepped onto the porch. "It's your battery. Stop trying to crank it, or you'll make it worse. I'll jump the battery."

Abby leaped out, looked at her wristwatch, and slammed the door. "Stupid car. I have to be in class in thirty minutes."

"Just take Sabine's car. I'll get yours running again and you can come pick it up this evening."

Hank fetched Sabine's keys and stood on the porch watching Abby adjust the seats and mirrors.

"What a morning," he muttered as she drove away. He stepped into the foyer and studied the family photos that hung there. The faded photo of his and Sabine's wedding day hung in the center, with the other photos in a pattern around it like planets frozen in orbit. Through thin films of dust, the faces of his parents, his brother JD, his sister Tracy, and his children stared back at him. Fishing trips, graduations, family reunions, baptisms. Hank glanced at his own bruised and swollen face, in the mirror, but his gaze returned to his and Sabine's wedding photo and then to the iPhone.

"Honey," he said, "I wish you were here so I could talk to you about this."

When he figured Abby had driven far enough away, instead of jumping off her car, he called Pete.

"Can you take off the rest of the day?"

"Most likely," Pete said, "seeing as how I own the place. What's so important?"

"Come over and I'll tell you about it."

While he waited for Pete, he tried to jump-start Abby's car to no avail. It was probably the alternator. *As if I don't already have enough to do today.* He put his jumper cables away, dressed in tactical pants and a sweatshirt, and stepped downstairs just as a cab deposited Pete in front of the house.

Pete limped up the walkway and smiled when he saw Hank's face. "You look like a side of beef that's been out of the cooler too long."

"You should see the other guy."

Pete eased into Hank's recliner with a pen and notebook while Hank sat upright on the couch.

"You got a lead on a bad guy?" Pete said, leaning his head back to look at the ceiling. "Sort of like old times, huh?"

Hank placed the cracked cell phone on the coffee table.

Pete looked at it and whistled. "That's one heck of a lead, amigo. How'd you get it?"

"I wrestled a psychopath on broken glass. Anyway, we need a Faraday bag to protect the phone and Cellebrite software to break into it and exploit the data. The problem is that we don't have either of those."

"You want me to buy the bag?" Pete asked. "I can make it look like I'm buying it for the restaurant."

"That would take too long. And it might arouse some unwanted attention. I'll improvise the Faraday bag from my old grill. The real showstopper is the software. We can't buy Cellebrite because we're not a law enforcement or intelligence agency. We'll have to use whatever software we can scrounge to pull the call data. If I could get my hands on Teeltech software, that might work nearly as well as Cellebrite."

"You want me to check around with some of my old buds?"

"No. Teeltech sells their phone-cracking software only to law enforcement."

Pete sighed. "Surely somebody—"

"Litton," Hank said. "I'll bet Litton can get me a pirated version of Cellebrite. It won't be as good, and it may have malware embedded, but ... it would work. I can install it on my old laptop. That thing's just a paperweight now anyway."

"After that?" Pete asked while he scribbled on the notebook.

"After that we go for a drive in the country. My old grill won't just be our Faraday bag, it will also be part of our cover."

Pete laughed as he scribbled. "Told you it was just like old times."

"We'll need picnic supplies," Hank continued. "Brats, sauerkraut, pickles, and mustard. We'll also need a Mac cable. My old laptop already has Microsoft Excel on it. Hmm. I want you to bring a video camera as a backup in case something goes wrong. Capture as much of the call data as possible on video."

"Um, I do have a question, what's with the grill and picnic supplies?"

"My old grill is made of stainless steel, so we'll line it with a plastic trash bag and use it as our improvised Faraday bag. Still, I'd prefer to be in an area with no cell service. Ever been to Raven Rock State Park up near Sanford?"

"Yeah."

"Let's check the website to make sure they're open today. Raven Rock probably has the right combination of low population density and steep terrain that will block cell phone signals. Our best bet is near the bluffs, but we can't take a huge picnic basket down there. We'll try the — aahh!" Hank tried to stand, but he sat back down and groaned in agony.

"What's wrong?"

"My ribs. I have to remember to avoid sudden moves."

"Hank, you don't look so good. Maybe you should rest a day or two before we do this. We're not young men anymore."

"We're going today. Right after we go see Sabine, in fact."

"I figured you'd want to go there first."

Hank grimaced and took a slow breath. "As I was saying, we'll try the parking lot at Raven Rock first. Until then, the SIM card stays out of the phone, and the phone stays powered off. One more thing, Pete."

"What's that?"

"Could you drive my truck? I'd really like to take another pain pill. Maybe two."

Hank sat at Sabine's bedside, reading Psalm 25 in a low whisper, aware that Samantha was watching him. He finished reading and watched her, the pain in his side briefly interrupting his breathing. He prayed silently, but as he closed his prayer, Sabine's lips moved. Hank stood too quickly, winced from the pain, and placed his ear against her lips. He waited, straining to hear. She made no sound but moved her hands as if washing them. Her fingers twitched and then lay still.

God, please let her wake up. Hank stood at her side for what seemed like hours, but it had only been two minutes by the clock on the wall. He knelt beside her and prayed for a few minutes more. When he rose to leave, Samantha smiled at him.

"I'm beginning to think she just might make it," she said. "She's moving her hands."

"I'm beginning to think so, too," Hank said. "I'm beginning to think so."

Continued in book two of the Hank McCaskill
thriller trilogy, "Flames and Mirrors."

ACKNOWLEDGMENTS

First, I thank God for giving me a little bit of writing talent and boat-load of stubbornness. I set out to write a novel, and with His help, I did. Along the way, I experienced my own hero's journey consisting of a call to adventure, refusal of the call, and acceptance of my quest. Along the way, I met allies and foes, gatekeepers, and mentors. And then, in the dark of night, I fought with the ultimate bad guy: my own fears. I quit work on this novel twice: once for six months and once for about three months. Both times, God rekindled in me the passion to finish it. Otherwise, I never would have pushed through those dark days.

To my wife Michelle and my family, thank you for putting up with me as I learned how to write. It was not an easy journey for any of us.

To my writing coach, Jaden Terrell, I give a huge thank you. Your comments and insight not only helped me write my book, but they also helped me develop my skills as a writer. To Larry Brooks, author of Story Engineering, thank you for your direct and clear criticism. Your input spurred me to learn my craft thoroughly before taking this book to market. The three editors I worked with, Ford McMurtry, Hank Henley, and Michael Douglas, also have a huge stake in this book. Ford offered suggestions that smoothed the flow of the story while letting me retain my voice as the author. Hank's comments on story consistency and dialogue made my story shine. And then there's Michael Douglas of MDM Media. Michael's meticulous line editing and fact checking ensured my novel was ready for commercial publication. I have never worked with a more detail-oriented and conscientious editor. Finally, I owe a special thank you to Margie Fields, who proofread my manuscript and spotted errors that somehow slipped through.

No novel would reach publication without beta readers. My beta reading team consisted of Del Stewart, Greg Wilkie, Martha Duke Anderson, Michael Henderson, Carol Christopher, Jack Marshall, and my brother Bret Whitmire. Like my editors, you not only shaped this novel, but you also shaped me as a writer. Thank you all.

To Paul Schad, Andy Garret, Don Dechert, Greg Wilkie, Carol Christopher, and my sons William and Brendan Whitmire, your expertise helped make this novel more realistic. Thank you.

Every author needs encouragement, and my friends Bill Brown, Jon Hood and John Gunter; my son Matthew Whitmire, and my cousins Brian Whitmire and Doug Whitmire provided that. Thank you for encouraging me even when I doubted myself. Doug, your passing in 2021 left a huge hole in my heart, but my memories of you encourage me to keep writing.

To my fellow authors Don Keith, Cap Daniels, Craig Price, William H. Brown, Jaden Terrell, and Logan Ryles, your acts of mentorship might have seemed small to you, but they made a huge difference to me. Thank you. I am indebted to you all, and I will pay it forward.

To all the good folks at the Wiregrass Writers' Group, thank you for keeping this group alive, positive, and productive.

Finally, to K.M. Weiland, Jane Cleland, and Savannah Gilbo, your podcasts, books, and courses were worth every penny. Thank you for all that you do.

ABOUT THE AUTHOR

Warren Whitmire is a retired Army intelligence officer with over 25 years in uniform followed by ten years' experience as a civilian intelligence analyst. Warren has provided intelligence support to both conventional and special operations units, as well as Army Aviation units and Air Force units.

Warren has a B.A. in Economics and is trained in intelligence analysis, counterintelligence, and forensics. He currently lives in rural Alabama with his wife and four rescue dogs. His hobbies include kayaking, fishing, history, music, and creative writing. He is active in his church and volunteers with an environmental group that promotes responsible use of Alabama's water resources. Warren works part-time as a computer simulations operator.

"Only the Dead" is Warren's debut novel and the first novel in the Hank McCaskill trilogy.